"I have absolutely no interest in hearing about your expertise or exploits as a lover,"

Jan exclaimed. "And I didn't hire you for your advice."

Anger flashed across his ruggedly handsome features, then vanished into something even more dangerous. "That's right. You didn't hire me for my advice," he agreed. "Just my body."

Jan was tautly aware of the force and strength of his powerfully masculine body almost touching hers. She turned, edging away from him. A strange expression flickered across his face. "Perhaps the best thing that could happen to you would be if I *did* make love to you tonight."

"How dare you!" Jan gasped. In a furious reflex action her hand flashed toward his face with deadly intent. They struggled silently for a moment until his greater strength and weight forced her backward across the bed. He tangled one hand in her hair, and his mouth covered hers in a deep, bruising kiss.

"Do you think you'll be so quick to forget this?" he asked with soft menace.

"I'm going to try!"

"You'll remember," he murmured with assurance

D0686516

Dear Reader:

As the months go by, we continue to receive word from you that SECOND CHANCE AT LOVE romances are providing you with the kind of romantic entertainment you're looking for. In your letters you've voiced enthusiastic support for SECOND CHANCE AT LOVE, you've shared your thoughts on how personally meaningful the books are, and you've suggested ideas and changes for future books. Although we can't always reply to your letters as quickly as we'd like, please be assured that we appreciate your comments. Your thoughts are all-important to us!

We're glad many of you have come to associate SECOND CHANCE AT LOVE books with our butterfly trademark. We think the butterfly is a perfect symbol of the reaffirmation of life and thrilling new love that SECOND CHANCE AT LOVE heroines and heroes find together in each story. We hope you keep asking for the "butterfly books," and that, when you buy one—whether by a favorite author or a talented new writer—you're sure of a good read. You can trust all SECOND CHANCE AT LOVE books to live up to the high standards of romantic fiction you've come to expect.

So happy reading, and keep your letters coming!

With warm wishes,

Ellen Edwards

Ellen Edwards
SECOND CHANCE AT LOVE
The Berkley/Jove Publishing Group
200 Madison Avenue
New York, NY 10016

TARNISHED RAINBOW
JOCELYN DAY

**A SECOND CHANCE AT LOVE
BOOK**

CHAPTER
One

JAN MCFARLAND CLUTCHED the red velvet rope to maintain her balance as a bulky woman in purple jostled her from behind. The discreet line of restraint meant to keep people from touching the paintings on exhibit teetered precariously, and another jolt sent Jan plunging toward a luminous swirl of blue and gray titled *Legacy of Dawn*. A strong arm shot out of the crowd and yanked her back, a last-minute rescue from certain disaster.

"Thank you!" Jan said a little breathlessly. She rotated her shoulder tentatively. The rescue had been timely, but not exactly gentle.

"Did I hurt your shoulder?" The husky voice held a note of concern. He moved slightly, making a protective barrier of broad shoulders between the flow of the crowd and her slim body. "There are some chairs in the other room, if you'd like to sit down for a few minutes."

"No, I'm fine. Really. And thanks again. I don't think I could afford the cost of ruining one of Mr. Bertanoli's paintings."

Jan smiled up at her rescuer, her brown eyes widening slightly as she realized he was one of the most strikingly handsome men she had ever seen. Thick, crisp hair that was somewhere between bronze and gold. Burnished tan. Eyes with the blue intensity of a Caribbean lagoon. Strong, angular jawline. She was too close to him to see his physique beyond the powerful shoulders, but in the press of the crowd their bodies were crushed together in an almost brazen intimacy. She could feel the hard muscles of his lean thighs through the lightweight material of her jade-colored, wool-jersey dress. The level of her dark-lashed eyes, in dramatic contrast to the pale gold of her hair, just reached his chin, where she could see the pulse beating rhythmically in the solid column of his throat above his classic black tie.

"I didn't realize there would be such a crowd here." She felt suddenly flustered by the enforced intimacy and the open interest in his blue eyes, and the words came out with an adolescent breathlessness.

"Bertanoli is becoming very popular. He has a particular talent for capturing the many moods of the sea." He did not appear flustered. If anything, there was a sudden hint of amusement in the small flicker of his mouth. "Are you an art collector?"

"Oh, no. But if I were, I'd scoop up *Legacy of Dawn*. It's a beautiful painting."

"You live here in Los Angeles?"

"No. I recently moved to Ventura from Phoenix, Arizona. I just drove into L. A. to see the exhibit this evening."

"Oh?" His eyes roamed her heart-shaped face with an underlined interest. "You're alone?"

Before Jan could decide on the advisability of admitting to a stranger—even as attractive a one as her rescuer—that she was alone, a female voice interrupted.

"Oh, Logan, there you are! I've been looking all over for you. Anton is waiting for us."

Jan was too petite to see the owner of the voice in the crowd, but her temporary companion lifted a hand in acknowledgment. He was scowling slightly as he looked back at Jan. His glance flicked across the crowd to the woman Jan couldn't see, then returned to Jan once more as if he were trying to make up his mind about something.

"You're sure your shoulder is all right?" he asked finally. It was obviously a question preparatory to leaving her and rejoining the woman who had called to him.

Jan smiled, hiding a twinge of rueful disappointment. Such a virile, attractive man inevitably would be with some woman, of course. From the proprietary sound of her voice, probably a wife. "Yes, I'm fine. And thanks again."

She watched as his broad shoulders forced a not impolite but decisive path through the crush of people. She had a vaguely let-down feeling as she let the flow of the crowd carry her on through the corridor of velvet ropes. The paintings were superb. They caught the sea in moods ranging from playful to tempestuous, stormy to serene. But for all their power and sensitivity, they couldn't quite hold Jan's attention, and her gaze kept wandering across the crowd, searching lightly for that commanding figure.

Finally she caught a glimpse of him, his head tilted attentively toward the tall woman at his side as they studied a painting together. The woman's back was to Jan, but there was something vaguely familiar about that regal stance and elegant silver-blond hair.

Jan was puzzled. She knew no one in Los Angeles. How could the woman look familiar? Yet the feeling persisted. By now Jan was barely looking at the paintings, magnificent as they were. Her attention was riveted on the striking couple across the room. Once the man touched the woman's elbow with a lightly protective gesture as someone crowded too close. Even across the room, his bronzed good looks stood out in the crowd. He was wearing a perfectly cut black dinner jacket that emphasized his Greek-god coloring and physique. Once the woman said something 'to make him laugh, and Jan's pulse gave an unfamiliar little flutter as his teeth made a good-humored flash against his tanned skin.

Jan tried to feel a superior bit of disdain for his impressive good looks. He was almost *too* handsome, and she had met enough handsome men in various spots around the globe to know that they were too often egotistically self-centered, too often looked on women as potential marks on a score-board.

Yet she had to admit there was a certain commanding presence about *this* good-looking man that went beyond ruggedly handsome face and powerful physique. He had an aura of controlled but simmering energy, a look of money and background and authority. There was also a hint in the way he handled himself in the crowd that beneath the flash-ing smile and California tan lay a hard core of tough, self-reliant character. She already knew he was quick-thinking and fast-acting. His instantaneous response to her nearly disastrous plunge toward the expensive painting had proven that.

Jan lost track of the couple when an elaborately hatted woman crowded in beside her. Disappointed, Jan made her way to the room where coffee and minuscule slices of cake were being served. She decided to forgo the refreshments and was heading toward the exit when she stopped short. The man's back was to Jan now, the woman facing her.

Jan could see now that the woman was considerably older than she had looked from the back. A good ten or twelve years older than the man's thirty-four or thirty-five years. Too many deep suntans over the years had weathered her face to mahogany, but she was still elegantly attractive in a lean, no-nonsense way. The light caught the glitter of diamonds at her throat and ears. And she still looked oddly familiar . . .

Recognition came to Jan with a jolt. Rue Farrington, that's who the woman was! Rue Farrington, president of the development corporation for which Jan's roommate, Shelley Wineteer, worked in Ventura. Shelley had pointed out Mrs. Farrington at the office a few days ago, when Jan stopped by to pick Shelley up for lunch. There was presently no *Mr*. Rue Farrington, so Jan's first impression that the voice calling "Logan" had belonged to a wife was evidently wrong. Did that mean . . . ?

Jan's startled gaze returned to the man's broad-shouldered back, slanting down to lean hips. He couldn't be . . . but he was! He fit Shelley's description down to the last bronzed, blue-eyed, hard-muscled inch.

Jan's first astonishment changed to disappointment mingled with a flash of scorn. All that look of character, of well-bred background and commanding authority, was nothing but a cultivated, pretended *act*. He was a phony from the top of his impressive height to the soles of his expensive shoes.

Jan suddenly realized she was standing dead-center in the room, literally staring at the couple, and drawing some rather odd looks herself. Hastily she moved to the damask-covered table and accepted coffee from a silver urn. She carried the styrofoam cup to a corner from which she could watch without being so conspicuous.

She observed the man from a new perspective now. He was very good at what he did, she decided cynically, in part because he didn't look like what he was. In spite of his almost brazen masculinity, he managed to convey the image of a youthful, dynamic president of some international corporation. Or a private investor discreetly handling old family money. An image Jan herself would have accepted at face value, if she didn't know differently. He treated Mrs. Farrington with just the right touch of protective deference, complimenting her elegance with his own golden good looks and air of money and breeding.

And, in truth, he was nothing but a paid escort capitalizing on his devastatingly handsome face and virile physique! A "gorgeous hunk" as Shelley had gigglingly described him. No wonder he had cut short his conversation with Jan when Mrs. Farrington beckoned. He was *on duty*.

The startling revelation about Mrs. Farrington's private life had come out the same day Jan had glimpsed Mrs. Farrington at the office, which was also the day the unsettling letter from Bakersfield had arrived. Talking to Shelley, Jan had skimmed lightly over the awkward situation the letter presented. She had laughed at herself, actually, for feeling self-conscious about attending a wedding alone in this age of women's lib. But she felt uncomfortable and self-conscious about it just the same, once she knew that Paul Callison was going to be there.

"You could always do what Mrs. Farrington does, if you don't want to go alone," Shelley had said with her impish grin.

"What's that?"

"Hire an escort."

"You can't be serious!" Jan gasped. "Mrs. *Farrington—?*"

"Hires herself an escort when she needs one." Shelley nodded her head vigorously for emphasis. "And if she ever finds out I told you, she'll probably have us both shot at sunrise. It is *very* confidential information."

Jan ignored the dramatics. Nothing Shelley got hold of was confidential for very long. Tidbits of gossip practically bubbled out of her. "But why?" she asked.

Mrs. Farrington was twice divorced, perhaps a bit past her prime, but still extremely attractive. To say nothing of wealthy and powerful. Why should she *pay* for an escort?

Shelley explained. Mrs. Farrington did a great deal of traveling on company business and disliked social situations in which someone felt obliged to furnish an extra man for her. Even worse was when she received an unwanted sexual pass that complicated business dealings. So she simply had taken to contacting a reliable escort service in each city to which she traveled, and hiring an escort when one was needed. This was, if not common knowledge, at least not death-at-sunrise confidential. The real secret was that she occasionally extended the practice to social functions around Ventura and L. A., discreetly hiring the men from a reputable escort service in Los Angeles.

Jan could understand the practical aspect of hiring an escort on out-of-town trips. A suitable paid escort could be a handy protective device and eliminate various awkward situations. It was something to remember if she ever found herself in a job where she traveled alone. But to actually hire a *date* . . .

Usually Mrs. Farrington chose older conservative-businessman types, Shelley added, but a couple of weeks ago Shelley had seen her in Santa Barbara with a "gorgeous hunk." Later Shelley found out the man was a hired escort because the bill, though marked "personal," had accidentally been routed across her desk.

Shelley laughed again, but then she wrinkled her pert nose in a small grimace of distaste. "He was one gorgeous hunk of man, but it would be kind of awful to *pay* a man for companionship, wouldn't it?"

Jan made a noncommittal sound.

"But maybe there are fringe benefits for a rich older woman who hires an escort." Shelley giggled and waggled her eyebrows up and down in an exaggerated leer.

Jan had laughed too, at the time, but just now, looking at the man named Logan with Mrs. Farrington, Jan's cynical thought was that he was probably quite adept at supplying any "fringe benefits" a client desired. However, Mrs. Farrington certainly did not look as if she found the situation distasteful. She appeared supremely elegant and self-confident.

As Jan watched, Mrs. Farrington and her escort were joined by a stocky, dark-haired man with rather nervous mannerisms. Jan recognized him from the photograph in the Ventura newspaper as the artist himself, Anton Bertanoli. There was something odd about his right arm, a rigidity in the way he held it bent and close to his body. A moment later, Jan realized that his hand was heavily bandaged, though it was done in a discreet dark color to blend unobtrusively with his suit.

Bertanoli talked to the couple with a kind of nervous effusiveness, gesturing now and then with his left hand. No doubt he was anticipating an important sale, Jan thought. He had better concentrate on Mrs. Farrington and forget her companion, she added scornfully to herself. Or did paid escorts make enough money to afford fine art, too?

Partially concealed by a potted bamboo, Jan sipped her coffee and considered the trio reflectively. Would she have the nerve to do what Mrs. Farrington was doing? The question was merely rhetorical, at first, and then a small shiver tingled up her spine as it suddenly became real. Would she have the nerve to do what Mrs. Farrington was doing and hire an escort to accompany her to the wedding in Bakersfield?

No! What if she got caught? What if someone—someone like Paul—found out? She would be utterly devastated, totally humiliated. She would never be able to live it down. Paul would laugh at her—or, worse yet, feel sorry for her.

And how was he going to feel when she showed up at the wedding alone, she reminded herself unhappily. Alone and twenty-six, not only unmarried but without even an eligible man in tow. Jan wasn't usually in this manless state, but she had been in Ventura such a short time that she knew scarcely anyone beyond her roommate yet. Paul would be smugly certain that he had made the right decision in dumping her, that she didn't have what it took to be a rising young corporate executive's wife. He'd sit in the church, so complacent and superior, with his complacent and superior wife, who *did* have all the necessary assets and qualifications, at his side. Jan would huddle on a back pew feeling like the poor little match girl. But if she arrived with a man with the looks and style and self-assurance of Mrs. Farrington's escort . . .

No, no, the idea was simply too preposterous. Jan crumpled her cup and tossed it in a wastebasket. What Paul Callison thought or felt no longer mattered. She had gotten over him a long time ago. She also had to laugh at her own dismal image of herself. She was hardly the naïve, wide-eyed, slightly-too-plump girl Paul had dumped six years ago, let alone a pathetic little match girl. She had traveled all over the world, met royalty and movie stars, and she would attend the wedding with head held high, proud of her independence.

And yet none of that, she thought unhappily, would impress Paul nearly as much as would the presence of a handsome, successful man who obviously adored her. She kept telling herself that this small urge to impress the man who had crushed her with his rejection was just foolish pride. It was beneath her. And yet it was there. The image of seeing Paul's mouth drop open as she sailed into the wedding on the arm of a devastatingly attractive man was deliciously, almost irresistibly inviting.

No, not just *any* attractive man, she corrected, considering Mrs. Farrington's companion with a ruthlessly appraising eye. *This* man. Phony or not, he would be perfect. Absolutely perfect.

There was no way, however, that that tantalizing image could turn into reality, she realized ruefully, half-regretful, half-relieved. She could hardly sidle up to the sophisticated trio and ask how one went about hiring the services of the one who was the paid escort.

Jan watched the woman and two men a moment longer, then sighed and headed for the exit. At the door, she took one last, regretful glance over her shoulder. The whole idea was outrageous, but he really would have been so perfect.

With a small shock Jan saw Mrs. Farrington and the artist head toward a closed door marked *Private*. The escort was momentarily alone. Would she dare?

There was no time to consider pros and cons. With a sudden reckless impulse, Jan strode toward the most attractive man in the room. She paused before him, her honey-tan skin flushed and pulse pounding. There was a surprised lift to his eyebrows and then pleased recognition in his blue eyes.

"How is your shoulder feeling now? I've never thought of an art exhibit as a dangerous place, but perhaps I've underestimated the—ummm—inherent viciousness of art connoisseurs." He smiled, and there was a husky note of laughter in his voice, too.

"My—my mother always said I was accident-prone." With his warm eyes on her, appreciatively but not insultingly bold, Jan felt as if she might melt right through the straps of her slim-heeled sandals. They smiled at each other, and then he touched her arm lightly, pulling her out of the path of two chattering couples. The touch sent an unfamiliar giddy feeling rushing through Jan.

She took a deep breath, fighting down that oddly breathless, heady feeling he aroused in her. He might be wildly attractive, lethally handsome, and utterly charming. He might even make her heart bound in unfamiliar somersaults. But his companionship—or more—was available to any woman for a price. She straightened her shoulders and tried to put a coolly businesslike note in her voice.

"I wanted to talk to you about..." Out of the corner of her eye, Jan suddenly saw that Mrs. Farrington hadn't entered that private door after all. She had turned and was headed straight back toward them. Jan had intended to ask some discreet questions about how to go about hiring him, but now there was no time. Trying not to succumb to panic, Jan whispered hurriedly, "May I have your phone number?"

"My phone number?" The man looked surprised. His voice was normal. "Why?"

"Because I want to call you, of course!" Jan hissed frantically. Mrs. Farrington was only a few steps away now. "For next weekend, if you're not already busy."

His eyes registered something beyond surprise, and then a frown formed on his tanned brow as his gaze swept over her in swift and not entirely complimentary reappraisal.

Obviously, Jan thought, feeling dissected by that cutting gaze, this was not the way he usually did business. He hesitated a long moment, his blue eyes impaling her, then reached for his wallet and dug out a small rectangular card. From an inside pocket of the expensive jacket he produced a gold pen and scrawled some numbers on the back of the card.

Mrs. Farrington was looking on curiously now. The man made no effort to find out Jan's name and make introductions. He was merely looking at her, his handsome features carved into an expressionless mask. Jan jammed the card into her purse, mumbled an awkward thanks, gave Mrs. Farrington a weak smile, and fled. Even if Mrs. Farrington realized what was going on, Jan told herself, she didn't know Jan and couldn't connect any of this with Shelley's revelation of a bit of confidential information. Jan could feel the man's gaze like a hot iron branding her shoulder blades all the way to the door.

Outside, the February night air was almost balmy, with little hint of the well-publicized smog or pollution so often credited to the Los Angeles area. Jan took deep gulps of air, trying to quell the trembling dampness of her hands and a peculiar urge to giggle. When she reached her car she fished the card out of her purse and held it up to the dome light.

The calling card was a rich cream color, the name engraved rather than merely printed. *Logan G. Pierce*. Nothing else. Very discreet. The scrawled phone number had a bold masculine slant.

Jan felt a moment of heady exultation. Awkward as the situation had been, what she had just done was proof that she was no longer the unsophisticated woman Paul Callison had rejected six years ago. That woman would never have been able to carry off what she had just done.

But as she headed back up the coast toward Ventura, Jan's feeling of exultation wilted. Yes, she had Logan Pierce's phone number. But would she really have the nerve to call him?

The apartment was empty when Jan reached it. No doubt Shelley was out with her fiancé. Jan was relieved. She was still in a state of nervous excitement that would surely have aroused questions from Shelley if she had been home. Jan had already decided that this was not something she could discuss with Shelley. Shelley was sweet and fun, vivacious and generous, but she also couldn't resist sharing a bit of delicious gossip. Jan didn't care to have it spread all over town that the new local television personality had to hire an escort to attend a friend's wedding in her home town.

Jan made herself a cup of pink peppermint tea and tried to think cool-headedly about the situation. There were several things she didn't like about it. Unpleasant consequences if the truth did leak out, though that was a farfetched possibility if she were very careful and confided in no one. Deeper was her basic repugnance toward deception. She was not a deceptive person. Yet it wasn't total deception, she argued with herself. She'd dated several extremely attractive men, even collected a few passionate proposals— of marriage and otherwise. It was just that she didn't happen to have a genuine admirer available right *now*.

And then there were the awkward mechanics of the idea. Who picked up whom? When did she pay? And how much? Her past employment with Adele Meeker had been worth a fortune in experience, but Adele had been, to say the very least, frugal with dollars. And this unplanned vacation between jobs, plus the move to Ventura, had been expensive.

At least Bakersfield wasn't so far away; they could drive back the same night, after the wedding. There wouldn't be the awkwardness or expense of an overnight trip.

By the time she got to that thought, Jan shakily realized she was really considering doing it. She was really considering *paying* a man for his company for the evening!

And why not, she challenged herself recklessly as she eyed the phone the next morning. Men had been doing it practically since time began. The apartment was empty. It was Saturday morning and Shelley had gone shopping.

Jan paused with a hand on the phone. Maybe she should wait until Monday . . .

No, she told herself firmly. No procrastination. If she was going to do it, she had to do it *now*.

She set the card on the stand in front of the phone. She picked up the receiver and dialed briskly, momentarily nonplused to realize the number was not a long-distance call. What did that mean? The phone was picked up on the second ring. A masculine voice she instantly recognized said hello.

"Hello." Now what, Jan wondered frantically.

"Logan Pierce speaking." The crisp voice held a hint of impatience.

"Hello," Jan repeated, trying to fill the vacuum while she collected her thoughts. "This is Jan McFarland. I spoke with you briefly last night at the art exhibit."

"Oh, yes. The woman who asked for my phone number." There was a certain chill in his tone that first intimidated and then annoyed Jan. Who did he think *he* was to act so superior? She wished she could see his face. No, she didn't either. There was something about the warm blue-smoke depths of his eyes that sent her usually disciplined thoughts spinning. Except that at the moment, from the frost in his voice, she doubted that his eyes held much warmth.

"About next weekend," Jan began tentatively. "Do you have something already scheduled for Saturday evening?" She suddenly hoped almost desperately that he did have. Then she could just mutter her thanks, and hang up, and forget this whole preposterous idea.

There was a faint rustling of pages as he checked a calendar. "I seem to have next Saturday evening open." He sounded wary, but there was a hint of challenge in his voice as he added, "What did you have in mind?"

Jan swallowed, her throat suddenly desert-dry. "Is this your home or"—she paused, searching for a proper term—"or your business number?"

"Home."

"Perhaps I should call your business office and make the arrangements through them." What she had to know, of course, was how much this would cost, but suddenly the question seemed just too gross. She had no qualms about asking the mechanic what he would charge to repair her car. Or the dentist what it would cost to fill a tooth. But to discuss with a man what he would charge to take her out on a date was just too much. She knew if she didn't ask now, however, she'd never gather up nerve to dial another number and ask. "Uh...what do you...uh...charge?" The question came out a cross between a mumble and a croak.

"For what?"

Varying charges for varying services, Jan thought, squelching an interior ripple that bordered on mild hysteria. She also refused to let her mind wander curiously along the trail of wondering what those various services might be. She shifted the phone to her other ear and wiped a damp palm on her jeans.

"This would involve just a—a trip up to Bakersfield next Saturday evening. To attend a w-wedding, as my escort."

Jan tried to control the unexpected stutter. She thought she had conquered that nervous tendency long ago. "No extras."

"I see." There was a slight creaking sound, as if he had leaned back in a chair.

"We'd return here the same night, after the wedding. Oh, but you don't live in Ventura, do you? Or do you?" The call hadn't been long-distance, and she was too flustered to figure out what that meant. "I could drive you back into L. A."

"That wouldn't be necessary." His voice had an odd, not-quite-definable quality now. Something of a mixture of wariness and interest, and perhaps a touch of held-back laughter. Was he laughing at her nervousness, knowing this was her first time at this? "I live in the Ojai Valley."

"You do?" Jan couldn't hide her surprise. The Ojai Valley, northeast of Ventura, was an expensive rural area of beautiful homes surrounded by acres of oranges and avocados. And the small but elegant town of Ojai, some fourteen miles outside Ventura, was the location of the new television station for which she would soon be working. It wasn't the sort of area in which she would have expected a paid escort to live. But then, she thought wildly, what did she know about how paid escorts live? "I took a drive out through the Valley a few days ago. It's a lovely area."

Jan berated herself mentally for making inane conversation. The expensive beauty of the Ojai Valley had nothing to do with anything. And now she somehow had to get back to the matter of price again. "About your fee," she began determinedly. "I mean, if you're interested?" Her upward inflection left the question dangling, like a stray sock flapping on a clothesline.

There was a long, drawn-out silence before he said, "Yes, I'm interested." He sounded half-angry. No doubt she was a comedown from the elegant Mrs. Farrington. Mrs. Farrington undoubtedly did not stoop to asking questions about such mundane matters as fees. And the question still had not been answered.

Jan tried once more. "About your fee—"

"What are you prepared to pay?"

The question caught her off guard, as did the unconcealed challenge in his voice.

"I—I presumed there were set fees."

"What are you prepared to pay?" he repeated. "What is my company for an evening worth to you?"

More than I can afford to pay, Jan thought shakily. She hadn't even the most remote idea of what a paid escort normally received, of course. She should have pried the information casually out of Shelley, who had seen the billings. Evidently Logan Pierce made his own financial deals when operating independently of the escort service.

"One hundred dollars?" she finally suggested uncertainly. When there was no answer, she added, "And I'd pay for a meal, of course. And furnish the transportation." Jan hated the queasy feeling that she was haggling.

"That sounds satisfactory." Logan Pierce's voice was neutral now. "However, I'd prefer to supply the transportation myself. I have a fairly decent car. When and where should I pick you up?"

Jan automatically started to give the apartment address, then caught herself. The last thing she wanted was for Shelley to see and recognize the same "gorgeous hunk" whose companionship Mrs. Farrington had hired. She named a corner intersection a few blocks from the apartment and an hour that would give them sufficient time to make the drive to Bakersfield.

"Fine. Everything is settled then." He paused. "I am curious about one thing. How did you happen to know I was—available?"

Some of Jan's scattered poise had returned. "I'm afraid I'm not at liberty to reveal that information."

"I see." For one tense moment, Jan thought he was going to change his mind and back out, but then he added crisply, "I'll see you next Saturday, then."

"I think it will be a fairly elaborate wedding."

"I'll try to wear something appropriate."

His tone was dry, and then the phone clicked in her ear.

Jan set the receiver down with trembling hands. There, it
was done. The thing to do now was to put the wedding and
everything connected with it out of her mind until next
Saturday.

CHAPTER
Two

However, putting the Saturday-night "date" out of her mind proved extremely difficult for Jan to do, for several reasons. One was that she felt an uncomfortable, queasy sense of embarrassment and guilt for resorting to this deception just to prove to Paul that he'd underestimated her. Another was that an image of Logan Pierce's ruggedly handsome features kept popping into her mind at the most unexpected and disconcerting moments.

Then something happened that temporarily banished all thoughts of the wedding, Paul Callison, and even Logan Pierce from Jan's mind.

Jan's appointment with Warren Anderson, manager of the new television station, was scheduled for Wednesday afternoon. Mr. Anderson had, for all practical purposes, assured Jan that she had the job at the station. He had seen

17

videotapes of her performance as assistant on Adele
Meeker's show. He was also a personal friend of Adele's
and gave considerable weight to her enthusiastic recom-
mendation of Jan's abilities and potential. He liked Jan's
concept of a midday women's show. Jan's understanding
was that this final meeting was more or less a formality.

In Tuesday's edition of the Ventura newspaper, there
was a brief, stunning announcement. Warren Anderson,
manager of the television station in Ojai, had collapsed and
died of a heart attack at his home.

Jan was shocked. She had met Warren Anderson only
briefly when he interviewed her, at Adele's urging, while
he was in Phoenix. She recalled him as appearing to be in
robust good health, a warm, capable person with whom she
was looking forward to working. As sorry as she felt about
his death, she couldn't help but also feel a certain apprehension about what effect his death would have on her own
future.

Her apprehension proved well-founded.

Jan drove out to Ojai and showed up punctually for her
two o'clock appointment. The director of programming,
Bruce Gurley, had temporarily taken over Warren Anderson's duties, and everything appeared to be running smoothly.
He was polite but reserved, informing Jan that he was sure
she would understand that, under the circumstances, the
situation at the station was "unsettled." Until a new station
manager was hired or promoted—and Jan knew instinctively he was thinking of himself in that context—the station
could not commit itself to new staff or programming.

He made a casual comment that Jan found dismaying.
He referred to her new show as "Warren's baby," and there
was a distinct hint of disparagement in his tone. Anything
more would have been unseemly under the circumstances
of Mr. Anderson's very recent death, of course, but the
disparagement was definitely there. If Bruce Gurley became
station manager, Jan had the sinking feeling that her show
would never make it on the air. Jan was uncertain whether
his suggestion that she check back in a week or two and
make another appointment meant there was still the possi-

bility of a job, or whether it was just a polite way of getting rid of her.

Jan tried not to succumb to panic. She was obviously going to be out of work longer than she had anticipated, but she might still be able to get some lesser job at the station and work into a local show of her own later. If worse came to worst, Adele had many contacts and could help her find a job somewhere else. There was no need to panic.

Jan spent the next couple of days exploring Ventura and watching the Ojai television station, trying to get a feel for its programming. One woman on their local news team wouldn't last long, Jan speculated. Her voice was strident and she had a way of glaring almost belligerently at the camera. Jan had never done news, but she thought she could handle it, and an opening on the local news team was a definite possibility. But there was also an extremely attractive brunette who showed up on a couple of local news features, and Jan suspected that she could be powerful competition. The station lacked a good children's show, something Jan knew she would enjoy, though the career possibilities in that line were probably limited. But she would get her foot in *somewhere* at the station, she vowed determinedly.

On Saturday afternoon, shifting priorities temporarily and putting the job situation out of mind, Jan dressed with meticulous care for the evening wedding. She wore a two-piece raw-silk suit in a shimmery brown-gold color that brought out the golden flecks in her brown eyes and made her pale golden hair look almost ethereal. With it she wore a ruffled champagne-colored blouse and small gold earrings. The effect was discreetly elegant and utterly feminine.

Shelley asked curiously how Jan had decided to handle the situation with her ex-boyfriend at the wedding. Jan just shrugged and said she wasn't going to worry about it. She knew her answer left Shelley assuming that she was attending the wedding alone, and she carefully did not correct the impression. Shelley, watching with interest while Jan expertly applied her makeup, casually tossed out a bit of information she had learned at the office. Mrs. Farrington was a shareholder in the corporation that owned the Ojai television station. The information didn't seem to have any immediate bearing on Jan's job prospects, but she filed it away mentally for future reference. It meant that Mrs. Farrington might help select the new station manager, and that could affect Jan.

Jan left the apartment fifteen minutes before the time appointed to meet Logan. She parked her car in a shopping-center parking lot and walked to the corner, feeling absurdly conspicuous standing there, obviously dressed for a night out, with makeup that was also overly dramatic for the hour. A couple of cars slowed and several interested male glances appraised her. She kept her eyes resolutely remote and her expression aloof, but she felt jittery inside until Logan Pierce appeared. He did, indeed, have a "fairly decent car," a sleek white Ferrari. Again she was impressed with how well the escort business paid. Evidently the usual fees were considerably larger than he was earning this evening.

Logan got out and opened the car door for her—a gesture not many men made anymore, she reflected as she draped her jacket over the seat. Perhaps one of the minor fringe benefits of *hiring* your escort, she thought wryly.

She sneaked a look at Logan. If anything, he looked even more perfect for his role than she had anticipated. He was superbly masculine, self-assured, and handsome in a rugged yet suave way, the very image of wealth and success. The cuffs of his white silk shirt were turned back casually from his wrists, but an elegant black dinner jacket hung behind the seat.

"Do I pass inspection? I'll roll down my shirt sleeves and put the jacket on before we get to the church, of course."

Jan flushed as she realized that her surreptitious scrutiny had not gone unnoticed. "You look exactly right," she said honestly.

He shot her a brief, speculative glance as he wheeled the responsive car in and out of the busy weekend traffic. "Exactly right for what?" he asked bluntly.

"For my friend's wedding." Jan knew her answer was a lame evasion. In an attempt to divert the conversation, she added, "I'm not sure how late we'll be getting back."

"I haven't anything else planned for the weekend." He reached over and switched on the stereo, keeping it at a low, soothing volume. "You seem a little uncomfortable," he commented. She responded self-consciously by locking her fidgeting hands together in her lap. "I take it you're not in the habit of hiring an escort."

"No, not really."

"You're very attractive." His quick sideways glance was appreciative though impersonal. "I would think you'd have a ready supply of men eager to take you anywhere."

"I really don't know anyone around Ventura yet." Another evasion.

"That's right, you did say you had just moved to Ventura from Phoenix. Why did you come here?"

"I thought I had a job." Jan hesitated. "But I guess perhaps I haven't." She didn't elaborate. He looked curious, but he chose—at least temporarily—not to pursue the subject.

"Jan—may I call you Jan?" She nodded and he added, "Jan is short for—what? Janice?"

"Actually, it's . . . January."

"January." He repeated the name, nodding as if it confirmed something to him. "Very appropriate."

She didn't want to ask what he meant, but she was too curious not to. "Why do you say that?"

"You look like a 'January.' Beautiful and cool and blond. Aloof and reserved. Sophisticated and self-assured and determined. A dependable person who lives up to her New Year's resolutions, but isn't afraid to try something new and daring. Polished." He paused, then, with a small, wry twist to his chiseled mouth, added, "Like a piece of ice sculpture."

Jan looked down at her hands clasped rigidly in her lap, oddly affected by his brief, shrewd analysis. Except for the slightly caustic "ice sculpture" comparison, what he described was the image she had worked hard to attain. She wanted to be self-confident and successful and sophisticated. She wanted to be lovely and gracious. She wanted to be all the things she *wasn't* when Paul rejected her. Sometimes she felt she had achieved those goals, but other times she was afraid it was all just outward appearance, a fragile mask. Behind the mask she was still the same old Jan McFarland, uncertain, more shy than aloof, and quite unsophisticated. Why else, she wondered ruefully, would she feel it necessary to put on this little charade for Paul's benefit?

"Or is what I see just a hard outside shell?" Logan mused. "And the real January McFarland, somewhere down inside, is warm and sweet and a little scared. And very, very vulnerable." His voice was soft, as if it were a thought wafting on the music more than spoken words.

For no reason that she could clearly explain, Jan suddenly found herself blinking back tears. She looked the other way, watching the hills and groves of lemons and oranges roll by without really seeing any of it. What had made him say that? How had he managed to slice through her carefully created exterior image to the soft vulnerability underneath?

"Would you mind telling me just why you were so desperate to bring a man to this wedding that you were willing to hire one?" he asked quietly. "Somehow you don't seem the type to play some game, like making an old boyfriend or ex-husband jealous."

Jan shook her head. "No, it isn't that—"

"I could play my role better if I knew what the game was," he pointed out gently.

"It isn't a game," Jan protested. Then she sighed. "Maybe it is." She hesitated a long moment. The sleek car passed a truck smoothly. Logan was right, of course. He needed to know a little of the situation in order to help her pull it off successfully. "There will be a man at the wedding," she said carefully. "Someone I used to know. A long time ago, he...hurt me very deeply. We were engaged, but he was very ambitious and he decided I wasn't suitable wife material for a rising corporate executive. He married someone who...was suitable." Jan's voice was low and her words jerky. "I just didn't want him to see me at the wedding...all alone."

The words drifted into an awkward silence, but Logan reached over unexpectedly and squeezed her hand. Jan fumbled in her purse for a tissue. She wiped her eyes and blinked hard and tried to laugh at herself.

"Silly, isn't it? Just foolish pride, I suppose, wanting him to see me and think that perhaps he made a mistake. Because there I'd be, sophisticated and successful, with this handsome, rich, successful man by my side." Jan shook her head ruefully. "The more I talk about it, the worse it sounds. I'm ashamed of myself."

"Don't be," Logan said with surprising vehemence. "This guy sounds as if he deserves all you have planned for him. And a hell of a lot more, if you ask me."

Jan let out a tremulous breath, suddenly realizing that she had been afraid he would either condemn or laugh at her. That he did neither made her feel a quick outpouring of warmth for him. She suddenly felt as if they were joined together in a small, secret conspiracy, a conspiracy that unexpectedly had a certain zest to it.

"What would you suggest?" she asked lightly. "I've considered a few little things." She smiled and sniffed back tears at the same time. "Maybe flogging or deportation or blackmail. Perhaps a lifetime sentence of three meals a day of nothing but cold ceral. He hated cold cereal. But everything I thought of seemed too good for him."

Logan smiled at her unlikely punishments, but there was a serious note in his voice when he said, "He must have hurt you very deeply indeed."

Jan nodded. She could laugh and make a bit of fun about all that now. The wound had healed over. But memory of the long-ago pain still lingered.

"Are you still in love with him?"

"No." Jan's denial was firm. "I hadn't even thought about him for a long time, but then I got a wedding invitation from a girl I went to high school with . . ."

Quite unexpectedly, Jan found herself telling him everything, going way back to school days in Bakersfield, when she was in junior high and Paul a high-school VIP. She more or less admired him from afar in those days, and it wasn't until the summer she graduated from high school that they really got to know each other. He was going to

UCLA by that time, but he was at home for the summer, working at a fast-food restaurant. He started at the counter, but within six weeks was assistant manager.

They were inseparable that summer, and by the time he went back to the university in the fall, they were lovers. Jan had intended to go to college, too. She wanted to be an elementary-school teacher, though once she fell in love with Paul, all that really mattered was being his wife. As it turned out, neither dream had materialized.

Jan's younger brother, Mike, was nearly killed in a disastrous water-skiing accident that summer. The tragedy left him both physically and emotionally ravaged. With surgical and psychiatric bills, hospital, and rehabilitation costs, college for Jan was out of the question. Without complaint, she simply stayed on at what had started out to be a temporary summer job as billing clerk for a wholesale plumbing-supply firm, and did what she could to help her parents and Mike.

The other dream, of being Paul's wife, died later.

Their affair continued through his final two years of college. Jan understood and accepted that. His family was no more wealthy than her own, and he was struggling through school on a combination of partial scholarships, summer and part-time work, and government loans. She was proud to bursting when even before graduation he was chosen for an elite management training program with an important electronics firm back east. She thought they would get married when he graduated, but Paul stalled—though she didn't recognize it as a stall until much later. He said he wanted to get better established with the company before they married.

The following spring he flew out to the West Coast on business. Later she was to think bitterly that he hadn't even made a special trip to break the news to her. He just waited until he could combine it with a business trip. He also waited until *after* they had had sex. Then he told her.

He had the good grace to be a little uncomfortable about it. He stammered and stalled, hemmed and hawed, and talked about having outgrown Bakersfield. But he finally got it out. It wasn't just Bakersfield he felt he had outgrown. It was Jan also. He had come to the conclusion that she simply wouldn't fit in as a corporate executive's wife. She was "different" from the other executives' wives, and he was marrying a girl he had met back east, a Smith College graduate. Her father was head of the company's legal department.

"And so that was the end of our romance." Jan's palms were damp, but her eyes were surprisingly dry. It was the first time she had ever told anyone the complete story, right down to the last painful, intimate details. She had let everyone believe the decision to break the engagement was mutual. But telling it all was, oddly, a relief, like untying a knot within her.

"You're a very good listener." She felt a bit self-conscious that she had spent so much time pouring out her story to him. By now they were traveling along the main north-south interstate freeway not far south of Bakersfield. The plowed fields were still winter-bare, but a few wisps of cotton from last year's crop clung forlornly to a fence. "I suppose it's part of your job."

He smiled slightly but made no comment. "And so, if you're no longer in love with this guy—what did you say his name is? Paul?—how do you feel about him?"

"Paul Callison." Jan tucked the tissue back in her purse. She was over that brief tearful spell. "Actually, I suppose I have a lot for which to thank him," she said thoughtfully. "He made me take a good, long look at myself. And I saw a lot of room for improvement."

Logan's gaze flicked briefly over her slimly rounded figure and shimmering hair. He quirked an eyebrow questioningly. "Such as?"

"When Paul and I split up, I was a good twenty pounds overweight. I was dowdy and frumpy, and my only mental exercise was working a crossword puzzle now and then. I had a naïve get-married-and-live-happily-ever-afterward outlook on the future. Paul's company placed a heavy emphasis on the social skills, abilities, and appearance of their executives' wives, so Paul was probably right. He might never have gotten ahead with me as a wife."

"A corporation just hires a man. It doesn't own him. I don't believe his wife should be any of their concern." Logan's voice was surprisingly sharp. "I know I'd damn sure tell a corporation to go to hell if they didn't happen to approve of the woman I loved."

"Is there a woman you love?" The curious but irrelevant question popped out before Jan could stop it.

"No." He hesitated and then said briefly, "I was married once. A long time ago. It lasted about a year. Fortunately we both realized we'd made a mistake and got out before we did each other too much damage. I believe she lives on the East Coast somewhere, with a husband and family." He made a change of subject as deftly as he maneuvered across lanes to avoid a speeding sports car that zoomed by. "So you launched on a self-improvement project."

"More or less."

Reeling under Paul's rejection and criticism, Jan had dieted and exercised away the excess weight. She changed her hair from an out-of-date, straight, center-parted style to a lush cascade of casual curls and highlighted the natural sandy-blond color to sunlit gold. She took a modeling and charm course and learned to handle clothes and makeup and posture and voice. She realized that the job she had was a dead end and switched to the steno pool of a big insurance company where there was an opportunity for advancement. She took a steady flow of night classes, business courses to help her on the job, plus various courses in history, English, philosophy, and psychology to improve her general knowledge of the world. In the back of her mind was the idea that she would still like to work with children, but then fate, in the form of a fantastic and most unlikely opportunity, intervened.

Adele Meeker and her secretary were just passing through Bakersfield. That was before Adele had gone into television, although she was already well known for a style of book unique to her: a kind of combination cookbook, travelogue, and collection of intimate tidbits of celebrity gossip. However, her temperament was already peppery, and in a fit of pique with her secretary's spelling errors on a manuscript, Adele had fired the woman on the spot. Always impulsive, Adele immediately advertised for a secretary willing to travel. Jan applied and then recklessly accepted the job when it was offered.

The job with Adele opened a whole new world of travel, excitement, and glamour to Jan. Adele's books collected the favorite recipes of celebrities from all over the world. But what really sold the books were Adele's deliciously intimate revelations about the private lives of those celebrities, where and how they lived and worked and ate . . . and loved.

This went on for several exciting years, but then Adele's increasing problems with arthritis limited her travel. She turned to television, selecting Phoenix, Arizona, rather than the usual television centers, because the climate agreed with her. Her TV show was much like her books—bright, bubbly, and gossipy. She cornered for an appearance on her show any celebrity who ventured into the Phoenix area. If an outside celebrity was lacking, she brashly managed to turn someone local into one. Jan was her general all-around assistant, coping with a myriad of details.

Then, inevitably, Adele's arthritis reached the point where she had to give up the show, but not without doing all she could to help Jan advance and get a show of her own. "Reach for the rainbow," she advised Jan gaily. "You'll never find it unless you reach for it."

And Jan was reaching.

"This wedding is really rather irrelevant," Jan added. "I suppose I should have ignored it. But the bride was a good friend of mine in high school, and I told her I'd come before I had any idea Paul would be there. He's a cousin of the groom, but I can't imagine that he'd consider a family wedding important enough to come all the way out here for."

Logan nodded. "It does seem out of character."

Full darkness had fallen and the dim interior of the luxurious car had a certain cozy intimacy. Jan felt lulled and relaxed. When Logan asked a few casual questions about her job, she felt no hesitation discussing it with him.

"I was supposed to have my own program, a women's midday show, on the new TV station out in Ojai," she explained. "But the station manager, with whom I'd been dealing, died unexpectedly, and now I may not have a job at all." She wrinkled her pert nose ruefully. "The director of programming is managing the station temporarily. I had the impression he would like nothing better than to dump all the old plans and put in his own."

"Perhaps you could start out in some other position and get your own show later, when the situation has stabilized."

"That was my thought exactly, but—" Jan sighed. "I've had a fair amount of experience, both on and off camera, but actually I was just a glorified gofer. Sometimes Adele had me doing things like running out for the special tea she liked, or fixing the hem of her dress just before a show. And I don't have a university degree, which could be a big disadvantage if I have to compete for a job with people who do have degrees."

The lights of Bakersfield were just ahead now. Jan felt a small tingle of excitement that evidently communicated itself to Logan.

"Excited about seeing Paul again?" There was a small hint of disapproval in his tone.

"No. Just—excited. I haven't been back to Bakersfield since I took the job with Adele."

"Your family no longer lives here?"

"No. They moved to the Midwest to be near a special rehabilitation center and school for Mike. He's able to work now, but they decided to stay in that area. I fly back once or twice a year to visit." At the first city stoplight, Jan looked at her watch. "Would you like dinner before or after the wedding?" Self-consciously, suddenly reminded of their employer-employee relationship, she added, "I said I'd buy your dinner."

"I'd like just a cup of coffee. Perhaps we could find a drive-in, if that's okay with you."

Jan remembered a drive-in and directed him to it, pleased to find it was still there, though the name had changed. A teenaged waitress came on roller skates and Logan ordered the coffee. A nervous little buzz in Jan's stomach told her it was just as well he hadn't wanted to eat yet. Her earlier relaxation had tightened inexplicably as the encounter with Paul neared.

The waitress rolled up to the door with two coffees on a tray. Logan sipped his in silence. Jan looked at him curiously. His chiseled features had a moody cast.

"Is Logan Pierce your real name?" she asked tentatively.

"Yes, of course." He sounded surprised. "Why?"

"I thought perhaps you used a pseudonym for your . . . work. Like an actor or writer."

"No, it's my own."

"How did you happen to get into this"—she hesitated awkwardly, but she was too curious not to ask—"this line of work?"

"As a paid escort?" He gave her a lazy, speculative look, and she was aware of a dark gleam in his blue-lagoon eyes. "You mean, what's a nice guy like me doing in a job like this? I don't seem the type and all that?" His voice was amused, but it had an unexpectedly taunting undertone that was not entirely pleasant. Suddenly they seemed to be adversaries rather than conspirators.

"You seem exactly the type," Jan retorted. "Excessively handsome. Magnificently charming. Marvelously adept at drawing a client out and getting her to talk about herself."

"Touché!" he murmured with a wry grin. "Let's just say that the chance to get into this line of work presented itself and I couldn't resist taking the opportunity." His mouth twitched lightly. "Do you have ambitions toward rehabilitating me? Making an honest man of me and all that?"

Jan couldn't help laughing. "I think you're probably unsalvageable."

"This could be just a part-time thing with me," he suggested. "Perhaps in real life I'm a poor-but-honest bookkeeper desperately trying to earn extra money for my poor, widowed mother's operation."

Jan tilted her head. "*Are* you a bookkeeper, et cetera, et cetera?"

"No." He took a sip of coffee. There was laughter in his eyes, though Jan was uncertain whether he was laughing with her or at her. "Actually, both my parents are in fine health and live quite comfortably in L. A. They're in Acapulco on vacation right now."

Half-suspecting that he was making fun of her, Jan challenged, "Do they know what you do? Like tonight?"

"I imagine they know as much about what I do as most parents know about their offspring's activities. Does your family know what *you're* doing tonight? Hiring a—"

"No! And I'm not going to tell them—or anyone. And I expect you to keep this confidential, too!"

He nodded and dipped his head with exaggerated obsequiousness. "Should we be going?"

Jan glanced at her watch. "Yes."

She gave him directions, and moments later they were parking in front of the big stone church. Lights glimmered softly from the impressive old building. Jan swallowed, feeling a sudden tightness in her throat. It was the same church in which she had once thought she and Paul would be married. Other guests were already going inside.

Logan rolled down the sleeves of his shirt and fastened the cuffs with simple but elegant black onyx and gold cufflinks. He slipped the black tie around his neck with practiced ease.

Jan fumbled in her purse for mirror and lipstick and touched up the generous curve of her mouth. Logan borrowed a tissue from her to wipe a smudge from his black shoes. A strand of her hair caught on a loose thread of her ruffled blouse and he helped untangle it, his fingers surprisingly deft. She dug her gloves out of her purse and slipped them on.

There was an intimacy to the small gestures of preparation, and Jan felt the closeness of conspiracy again.

"Ready?" Logan asked. He paused, one hand on the door. "Don't be nervous. You look terrific. You're going to knock him dead."

"Well, I wasn't planning quite that drastic an effect," Jan said with a tremulous laugh, "but it might not be a bad idea." She swallowed nervously, her dark eyes unnaturally brilliant. "I feel like a fraud," she confessed.

He leaned across the seat unexpectedly and brushed his mouth against hers. The touch was fleeting, reassuring, and encouraging rather than passionate; yet it made Jan feel strangely breathless, and a little shiver tingled through her.

They walked up the steps of the church, Logan's hand cupping her elbow lightly. She knew they made a striking couple. Curious glances told her so. She felt the nervousness beginning to build to a heady excitement.

"What does this guy look like?" Logan asked in a low voice.

"He's tall. On the lean side. Brown hair. Intellectual-looking . . . but very good-looking." Suddenly she clutched Logan's arm. "There he is! Going into the church up there just ahead of us."

Logan nodded, his eyes following the gray-suited figure, and she felt a sharp tightening of his hand on her arm. She gave him a quick glance. He looked supremely sophisticated, totally self-assured, quite at home in the elegant clothes; yet he wore them with a certain careless disdain, as if he might be equally familiar with less civilized trappings. There was a dark glitter in his eyes, and the smile he gave her had a reckless flash. She was unexpectedly reminded of a film she had once seen, tense scenes of a panther stalking his prey in the jungle, and the errant thought occurred to her that not all predatory animals inhabited the jungle. Some prowled the streets of civilization in debonair disguise.

But they were no less dangerous.

CHAPTER
Three

THE WEDDING WAS traditional and lovely. The lighting was subdued, mellow with the golden glow of candlelight. The bride wore white satin and lace and a glow of happiness. The groom was properly proud, and the sweetly traditional ceremony brought an ache to Jan's throat and a brightness of tears to her eyes. She didn't realize until the ceremony was almost over that her fingers were entwined with Logan's hand, and she was holding on to him as if her life depended on it.

Surreptitiously she brushed a tear from the corner of her eye. "I don't know why I go all sentimental. Statistically, there's a pretty good chance they'll be divorced in a few years." She'd meant to make the comment cynically cool and worldly, but instead it came out tremulous. She didn't really believe it. Some marriages were forever. She thought this one was. She blinked rapidly to rid herself of another tear that threatened to slide down her cheek.

Logan's hands, lightly holding her waist until they could edge into the crowded aisle, gave her a quick, understanding squeeze. "What now?" he whispered, head dipped. She could feel his warm breath on her ear.

"Reception in the banquet room of a downtown restaurant."

"Do you see Paul?"

"No." She'd lost him completely in the crowd. There were more people at the wedding than Jan had anticipated. She probably could have attended alone and avoided seeing Paul completely, but she was glad Logan was there. He had a certain protectively gallant air that was vastly reassuring.

They made their way outside and then to the downtown banquet room. In the reception line, Jan and the bride, her old school friend Cindy Dodson, exchanged enthusiastic hugs. The groom, Paul's cousin, was friendly but didn't recognize Jan, which Jan took as an oblique compliment. Cindy discreetly did not say anything to jog her new husband's memory about Jan's past relationship with Paul. Jan introduced Logan, and Cindy was obviously impressed and curious. Jan just smiled mysteriously and didn't identify Logan beyond his name.

Beyond the reception line, they accepted glasses of champagne punch. Jan saw and spoke to a few people she knew. She got the same reaction several times. Someone would respond to her greeting in a way that said the person thought she looked familiar but couldn't quite place her. Then would come the flash of recognition coupled with a small double-take. Jan used the same routine that she had with the bride and groom, introducing Logan but not really identifying him. After several repeats of this, Jan found she was enjoying herself. She and Logan exchanged a warm, secret smile of conspiracy. He was by far the most impressive and attractive man in the room. There was a masculine strength and brilliance about him that drew female glances like a magnet.

And then she saw Paul. He was almost at the end of the

reception line. He hadn't changed much. Same lean height, same intellectual, slightly aloof expression. Brown hair conservatively but stylishly cut. Three-piece gray business suit. A woman stood ahead of him in the line, another behind him. Jan couldn't tell which of them belonged with him. In fact, it almost looked as if he were alone. Was he? Perhaps he had merely combined the wedding with a solo business trip to the West Coast. He was very efficient about things like that, Jan remembered with a certain wry bitterness.

Logan's gaze followed hers. "That's Paul?" Jan nodded. "What do you want to do now?" he added.

"Nothing." Jan's voice was low but firm. She had no intention of seeking Paul out. She had no desire to talk to him. This was all she wanted. For Paul, if he glanced her way, to see her slim and serene, impeccably groomed and dressed. *And not alone*. She tucked her hand around Logan's solid arm and resolutely turned her back on the reception line.

"He's headed this way." Logan's voice was low, his gaze over her head.

Female curiosity got the better of Jan. She deposited her glass shakily on the table. If Paul wasn't alone, she wanted a peek at the woman he had married. She turned, and her eyes met his as if the contact were planned. He stopped short. He didn't do the almost comical double-take several other people had, but his gray eyes narrowed in calculation. Then he stepped forward swiftly.

"Jan! How good to see you! You look—" He paused momentarily, seeming at an uncharacteristic loss of words. "You look lovely."

"Paul! I had no idea you'd be here." An outright lie, she thought guiltily. She was suddenly conscious of a hand resting lightly around her shoulders. She quickly made introductions, identifying Paul to Logan as an old friend from high-school days, but not explaining Logan to Paul. Without removing his left hand from her shoulder, Logan reached around Jan to acknowledge the introduction with a handshake. When he pulled his hand back, he rested it lightly on Jan's waist. She was enclosed in the protective semi-circle, his hard, muscled body pressed intimately against her back.

"What are you doing these days, Paul?" Jan asked brightly. She was aware that Logan's hand on her shoulder was edging toward her neck, and his thumb made a sensuous caress on the nape of her neck beneath the golden cascade of hair.

"I'm still with Twenty-First Electronics. I was recently promoted and transferred to the West Coast, as assistant supervisor for the area." There was pride in Paul's voice, but his eyes made a quick, distracted flick to Jan's throat.

Logan's strong fingers were lightly but openly caressing that sensitive area now, and his other hand slid around to the front of her waist, pressing her body back against his even more tightly. The intimacy of his gestures was hardly appropriate in this crowded gathering, and Jan knew the caresses were solely for Paul's benefit, but she couldn't escape a certain internal tug of physical reaction, an un-expected quickening of her pulse. She could feel the hard muscles of his thighs and the formidable breadth of his chest. Both spoke of physical strength, as did the hard grip of his hand on her waist, but that caress on the nape of her neck was infinitely lazy and sensuous. A caress, she realized with a small sense of bewilderment, that Paul couldn't even see.

"Twenty-First Electronics?" Logan repeated. "Isn't that the company that was involved in the congressional inves-tigation on bid rigging of government contracts a while back?" Logan's voice was innocently guileless, and Jan had no idea what he was talking about, but the comment brought a mottled red stain to Paul's face. How had Logan known anything about Paul's company?

"Our company was cleared of any wrongdoing," Paul said stiffly.

"Really?" Logan's tone was pleasantly skeptical. "I had the impression that the outcome was considerably less con-clusive than that."

Paul's throat moved in a convulsive swallow. His hands

were clenched so tightly at his sides that the knuckles stood out white and bony. And all the time that mesmerizing caress on Jan's throat continued, sending long tendrils of warmth curling deeper and deeper inside her. She had the strange feeling that, unless she made a special effort to keep control, her eyes might go all loose and unfocused, so intoxicating was the sensation of his touch.

"More or less cleared," Paul amended tightly, his eyes on Logan's hand. Paul's jaw jerked as he gritted his teeth. Then, sounding reluctantly curious, he voiced the question about which Jan had also wondered. "How do you happen to be familiar with Twenty-First?"

"Oh, I invest a bit in the stock market now and then. Too bad about the effect of the investigation on Twenty-First's stock price." Logan's words were sympathetic, but twisting in his arms, Jan saw that his brilliant smile was not, and the combination was somehow more devastating than an outright sneer would have been. Which was exactly the way Logan calculated it, Jan suspected. Paul was fidgeting with his collar, definitely uncomfortable.

"What line are you in?" Paul suddenly demanded belligerently of Logan. The air bristled with tension.

Jan's heart flip-flopped. She hadn't discussed this subject with Logan, and she had the sinking feeling that Paul had trapped her in her deception after all. She waited, poised helplessly, like the moment before a roller coaster begins its sickening swoop, waiting for Logan to flounder in some lie and Paul to smile knowingly.

"President of Pierce-Logan Enterprises. Family-owned corporation."

"Pierce-Logan?" Paul repeated doubtfully.

"It's confusing, I know," Logan said. "Logan was my mother's maiden name. We have interests in computers, TV and radio, some communications equipment." His voice was careless. "That and being on the board of directors of several other companies keeps me busy." Jan tilted her head enough to see him smile pleasantly.

Paul frowned and ran a hand across his jaw in a gesture that Jan remembered meant an iron exertion of self-control, almost as if the hand were meant to prevent the mouth from saying something inappropriate or incriminating. His expression was impressed but guarded.

"What companies?" he asked finally.

That really was getting a little too inquisitive, Jan thought indignantly, but Logan didn't seem to mind.

"Buenaventura Development Company. Pierce Communications." He named a couple of others negligently.

It took Jan a moment to realize that Logan had had the raw nerve to name Mrs. Farrington's company, Buenaventura, as one of those on which he held a directorship. Suddenly her tense nervousness evaporated, and she had to use her own willpower to control the laughter that unexpectedly bubbled within her like uncorked champagne. Paul was never going to outwit or trap Logan Pierce! Until now Jan's hands had been clasped nervously at her waist, but she reached up recklessly and entwined her fingers with Logan's, her eyes fixed innocently on Paul. She wasn't sure but she thought Logan's lips brushed a whisper of a kiss on her hair, and then his chin rested lightly on her temple as his arms slid down to completely encircle her waist from behind. It was all just a charade, a game, yet Jan felt dangerously light-headed. She had a strange, hungry impulse to turn in his arms and lift her mouth to his, never minding that this was neither the time nor place for that.

"Jan, may I speak with you alone for a moment?" Paul's unexpected request was abrupt, almost harsh.

Jan was too surprised to say anything for a moment, but Logan was not.

"I'm sure anything you have to say to Jan can be said to me also." Logan's quick answer was deceptively soft, because Jan could feel the hard tensing of his muscles, like a panther poised to strike.

Paul didn't move, but something about him suggested a certain wary retreat. His eyes slid from Logan's face to Jan's. "It's quite important," he said stiffly. "And personal."

Jan hesitated. What could Paul possibly have to say to her now that was "personal"?

Logan, his arms still around her waist, pushed back the

cuff on his left wrist to reveal a gold watch. "We probably should think about leaving, sweetheart, if we're going to make it back to Ventura tonight. Unless you'd rather spend the night somewhere along the way..."

His clean-cut jawline nuzzled her temple intimately, and Jan felt a small flare of indignation. His suggestive tone and words were going a little too far. He was implying to Paul that she and Logan might be spending the night together.

"Would you excuse me a moment, please?" Jan said crisply to Logan.

She abruptly slipped out of the possessive circle of his arms and walked to an empty corner of the room. Paul followed. Jan wouldn't put it past Logan to tag along arrogantly, but a surreptitious glance over her shoulder showed him simply standing by the punch table, a thoughtful expression on his handsome face. She was also amazed, and a little annoyed, to see that the moment Logan was alone, a lush brunette headed toward him as if she had been just waiting for an opportunity to pounce.

Jan wished she had thought to grab another glass of champagne punch. Her throat felt sandy dry, and she needed something to keep her hands from fidgeting. Instead she took a deep breath and made herself say calmly, if somewhat tardily, "Congratulations on your promotion, Paul. Are you pleased to be living on the West Coast again?"

If he heard the question, he paid no attention to it. He was looking back at Logan and the brunette. The girl was gazing up at Logan as if he were edible. "This guy Pierce—is he someone special? I mean, is there something serious between you?"

"Well, nothing definite," Jan murmured evasively.

"Jan, I haven't told this to anyone else yet—they all think Corrinne is planning to join me out here later—but we're in the process of getting a divorce." He spoke hurriedly, with nervous glances in Logan's direction, as if he suspected Logan might come charging over at any moment. "The only reason I drove all the way up here from L. A. for the wedding was in hopes I might see you. I'd heard through Cindy how you'd changed."

Jan was astonished. "Your mother doesn't know about the divorce yet?" It was a stall while she tried to collect her thoughts. Paul . . . divorced!

"I'll break the news to her this weekend." He gave another uneasy glance at Logan. He and the brunette were laughing together now as if they were old friends. Jan felt an almost unreasoning impulse to stalk over and do something blatant to stamp Logan as *her* property. Hands off. The thought was ridiculous, of course, and she forced herself to look back at Paul.

"Paul, what happened to the marriage?" she asked, honestly perplexed. "You seemed so *sure.*"

"It was just one of those things that didn't work out." Paul shrugged. "But a man ought to be warned never to marry the daughter of a lawyer. When divorce time comes, he knows all the devious little tricks and angles," Paul added with sour amusement.

"Paul, I'm so sorry," Jan said. "I'm really . . . shocked."

Paul turned away abruptly from his bitter inner thoughts. "But none of that matters now. It's in the past. What does matter now is *us,* you and me, and how unforgivably wrong I was about you. You're lovely, Jan. You're the most beautiful woman here tonight. Cindy told me you'd traveled all over with some writer, worked in television . . ." He shook his head. "I was so wrong, Jan. I just can't say it enough times. And I'm so sorry."

Jan hardly knew what to say or think. The outburst of compliments and apologies was so unlike Paul. He never apologized or admitted he was wrong, yet here he was coming to her almost abjectly.

"Do you have children, Paul?"

"A little girl. Corrinne gets custody, of course. You never married?"

"No." She added lightly, "I've been too busy."

"Jan, I was so hoping that we could get together for a good, long talk, that we could straighten things out and start seeing each other again." He shot Logan a dark look. "But I doubt we'll have the chance to talk with your possessive friend around."

Jan's thoughts were a tumultuous jumble. Paul divorced...free! Knowing he'd made a mistake about her, apologizing, coming here purposely to try to see her. The door that had slammed shut on her six years ago suddenly stood wide open again. Did she want to walk through, see what was on the other side?

No! one part of her shouted. Not after what he'd done to her, not after the way he'd hurt her.

Yet everyone made mistakes, she reasoned. That was why there were erasers...and divorce courts.

"Paul, I—I don't know."

"I was hoping you were planning to stay overnight here, so we could see each other tomorrow. I'm staying over at my mother's and driving back to L. A. tomorrow."

"Ventura isn't really very far from L. A."

"Yes! That's right." His gray eyes brightened. "If you could get rid of your friend, I could drive you home myself tomorrow."

That wasn't what Jan had meant. What she had meant was that, because Ventura wasn't far from Los Angeles, Paul might drive up and see her sometime. But the thought seized her now that she *could* send Logan on home, get a motel room, and stay over. She was a little unprepared, of course, but she could buy a toothbrush, rinse out her underthings.

"What about it, Jan? I know I could come up to Ventura and see you next week, but I feel as if we've wasted years, and I don't want to waste another minute."

In his eagerness, Paul seemed even to have momentarily forgotten Logan's forbidding presence nearby. His gray eyes, so often like silvered ice, had a smoky warmth.

"Paul, I just don't know! I mean—" She stopped as she felt a strong arm slide possessively around her shoulders.

"Darling, you've been gone a long time." Logan's voice was reproachful. His lips nuzzled her temple. "I missed you."

"Logan, stop being ridiculous," Jan said distractedly. "Something has come up. I—" She broke off, suddenly knowing instinctively that Logan wasn't going to approve of her staying over. Instead of coming out with a positive statement that she was staying, she finished rather lamely, "I'm thinking about staying in Bakersfield overnight."

Logan's blue eyes darkened like gathering storm clouds, but his voice was calm. "I don't think we can do that. I really should be back in Ventura fairly early tomorrow."

"I didn't mean we'd both stay. You could drive back to Ventura tonight. I could get a motel room, and then Paul would drive me home tomorrow."

"No. I don't think that's advisable." Logan's voice was casual but decisive.

Jan stared at him, uncertainty and uneasiness turning to anger. What did he mean—*no?* Then she remembered that Logan didn't know the current situation. He thought, as she had until just a few moments ago, that Paul was still married. She took a steadying breath. "Logan, Paul and I have some important and personal things to discuss. Paul and his wife are separated and in the process of getting a divorce."

If she thought that news would suddenly make Logan agreeable to a change in plans, she was mistaken. He merely flashed Paul a sardonic smile.

"Too bad."

The comment was so unsympathetic that Jan might have been mortified, or amused, under different circumstances. As it was, the smile and caustic comment only increased her annoyance. Up to that point she hadn't definitely made up her mind to stay. It was just a tenuous thought that it *could* be done. But Logan's arrogance, his unspoken attitude that he knew what was best for her, clicked the decision into place. She had hired him and she could *un*hire him.

"Well, I am staying," she said defiantly, "so—"

"I brought you here and I'll take you home. If you're staying overnight, so am I."

She half-turned, still caught in his powerful grip, to look up at him, dismay and surprise and anger all tossed together on her face. She had the panicky feeling that she had grabbed onto a dangerously powerful force and couldn't let go. A certain wicked gleam in his eyes told her that she might have hired Logan Pierce, but that didn't necessarily mean that she had even a whisper of control over him.

Jan's frustrated glare darted back and forth between the two men. For a moment, the contrast was almost brutal. Next to Logan's bronzed good looks and powerful figure, Paul looked pale and bland, thin rather than lean. Jan banished the thought quickly. Paul might not be as impressively handsome as Logan, but he didn't trade on his looks or a lot of phony charm either.

They seemed to be at a stalemate. The stalemate was prolonged, not broken, by a sudden flurry in the crowd. The bride was preparing to cut the three-tiered wedding cake. Flashbulbs popped as the groom's hand covered the bride's to make the first cut. Then she fed him the first bite, smudging frosting on his face as her hands trembled with charming bridal nervousness.

Logan had moved around behind Jan and had both arms intimately clasped around her again, his hands locked at her waist. The embrace that had earlier been amusing, even tantalizingly exciting in some unexpected way, now merely infuriated her. She tried to move away from him, but his grip was velvet-encased steel.

The little flower girl suddenly peered out from under the table, and her small hand mischievously reached up to pluck a frosting rose from a piece of cake.

"Oh, look," Jan said brightly. "Isn't she adorable? Is she a relative of yours, Paul?" Paul had to turn and look, and Jan used the small diversion to give Logan an awkward backward kick, an action that she unhappily suspected hurt her heel more than it did his shin. "Will you please let me *go?*" she hissed in a furious whisper. "And I don't want you staying here all night."

"Sorry. I never leave a job without seeing my client safely escorted home." His lips brushed her ear as he whispered into it, and Jan was all the more infuriated because the touch sent an unwanted wave of erotic awareness rippling through her. "Professional ethics and all that, you know." The whisper held a certain malicious amusement, yet there was an undertone of deadly seriousness.

"If your fee is what you're worried about, I'll pay you the amount we agreed on whether or not—"

"I think she's from Cindy's family." Paul turned back, a suspicious look on his face as he caught them whispering in short, furious bursts.

Jan was so distracted that it took her a moment to realize what Paul was talking about, to remember that she had asked about the flower girl.

The cake was served. Jan accepted a slice only because it gave her a chance and reason to slip out of Logan's stubborn grasp. He was behaving utterly outrageously, she thought angrily. Why was he doing it? What if she couldn't get rid of him? She'd have to ride back to Ventura with him tonight and assume Paul would contact her later.

She glanced up to find Logan looking at her with a secret, knowing expression. Amused. And what did *that* mean? She felt like kicking him again, and this time making it something more than that ineffective little backward jab.

No, she would not go back to Ventura with him tonight, she thought furiously. She had no obligation to him. If he chose to stay in Bakersfield tonight, that was his business. But she would not let his insolent arrogance interfere with what she wanted, and that was to see Paul tomorrow and talk to him and find out if anything remained of their old love.

The too-rich cake sat leadenly on Jan's empty stomach, and she suddenly felt a little queasy. Musicians were setting up for dancing, but dancing was the last thing Jan wanted when she had no idea what outrageous behavior Logan might think of next.

The three of them, a strange and uncomfortable trio, moved off to one side as waiters cleared the floor for dancing. Logan had one arm firmly clamped around Jan's waist again, his hand resting on her hip with easy familiarity.

"I think I'll run on out to my mother's place now." Paul looked uneasy but finally said to Jan, with a wary glance at Logan, "Can I give you a lift somewhere?"

Logan gave Jan no chance to answer. "I'll take care of it," he said smoothly.

Jan tried once more. "Really, Logan, there's no need for you to stay here overnight."

"Just part of my job." He smiled meaningfully.

Jan's eyes widened, and she felt a stab of alarm. There was a hint of threat underlying the casual statement, and she suddenly realized that Logan could make an utter fool of her in front of Paul if he chose to reveal their real relationship. And she suspected he was quite capable of doing exactly that. His small comment was just a warning.

"I'll call you in the morning and let you know where I'm staying," Jan said lightly to Paul.

Paul gave her another uneasy glance, as if he wondered how Logan was going to fit into all this. Then he nodded a reserved good-bye and worked his way through the crowd to the exit. Logan did not release his imprisoning grip on Jan.

"You can let go of me now," she whispered angrily. "The show is over. Paul is gone."

"What makes you think I was only doing it for Paul's benefit?" His fingers made a lazy caress over the curve of her hip, a slow, intimate gesture that ridiculously made her think of dreamy, leisurely hours of lovemaking...

"I'm afraid your thought processes escape me entirely," Jan muttered. She tossed her head with light defiance. "Now, if you'll excuse me, I'll find a phone and call a cab to take me to a motel."

"You don't care to stay and dance?" He looked innocently surprised.

"No, I do not care to stay and dance." Jan's words came through gritted teeth.

"And you definitely won't change your mind about staying in Bakersfield overnight?"

"No. I want to see Paul tomorrow."

"You can't be serious, Jan! After what he did to you—"

"He said he was wrong."

"Wrong about what?"

Jan hesitated, momentarily puzzled. "Wrong about me, of course."

"But not wrong about his attitude that it's fine to pick

a wife the way a corporation chooses an executive. Not wrong about the way he dropped you like an ill-fitting shoe. Jan, he's the same s.o.b. he always was, and you're making one hell of a mistake!" Logan stared down at her in angry frustration, then suddenly whirled her around, and marched her to the door as if she were an errant child on her way to the principal's office. "I'll take you to a motel."

"I can't leave without saying good-bye to Cindy."

Logan's mouth tightened, but he didn't argue. Jan half-expected him to be rude to Cindy and her new husband, or at least aloof, but he turned on the charm and captivated them. As they went outside Jan felt sourly as if they were *his* friends instead of hers.

The night was cool and crisp, colder than Ventura had been. Logan started the car. The mountains to the east loomed like dark waves of shadow.

"Is there some particular motel at which you'd prefer to stay?"

"No."

He drove the sleek Ferrari around the city streets with a controlled savageness, like an ill-tempered panther on the prowl. He said nothing except to ask curtly if she was hungry. She replied just as curtly that she was not, and he continued his prowl. He rejected several motels without explanation before pulling under the red-tiled canopy of a luxurious Spanish-style motel. Jan started to protest. It looked far more expensive than she could afford. Then she clamped her teeth on the protest, knowing that she had better accept whatever she could get. The uneasy thought had occurred to her that Logan could simply head for Ventura with her trapped in the car, and she would be powerless to stop him.

"Thank you for bringing me here," Jan said, stiffly courteous. "If you'll figure out what I owe you in addition to your basic fee . . ." She opened her purse. "And add on the cost of a dinner, of course, since that was included in our agreement."

"I told you, my job isn't over until I deliver you home.

And since you insist on spending the night here . . ." He left the sentence hanging as he opened the car door and swung his long legs out.

Jan hesitated, dismayed, and then she was jolted into action by a sudden suspicion of what he might do. She dashed to the heavy glass doors and reached the registration counter only a step behind him.

"We'd like two rooms, please!" Her voice sounded embarrassingly breathless even to her own ears. She felt foolish as Logan gave her a disdainful glance that suggested she was being presumptuous to think he would want to spend the night *with* her.

The desk clerk pushed a registration form across the counter. His bored expression said that he wasn't interested in whatever game they were playing. Jan fidgeted while Logan filled out the registration. The clerk set two keys on the counter. Logan seemed oblivious to her by now, but when she reached for a key, his hand closed deftly over both keys, keeping them out of her grasp. He completed the registration and paid for both rooms with a credit card.

Oh, very impressive, Jan thought scornfully. *Acting like the big spender.* And tomorrow the cost of both rooms would be tacked onto the growing bill she owed him.

They drove around to the far side of the court. Logan unlocked a room, reached inside to flick a light switch, and stepped back to let her enter.

The switch turned on a bedside lamp, and in its mellow glow the room was large and comfortable. Colorful pottery lamps, a bullfighter scene on the wall, and touches of wrought iron carried the Spanish decor inside. An elegant red plush bedspread echoed the red of the bullfighter's cape. There was a color television, a telephone on the nightstand, and an enameled hotplate with carafe for brewing morning coffee. And an enormous mirror. In the warm glow of lamplight the room had a sensual intimacy that Jan found unnerving in Logan's presence.

"Satisfactory?"

"Yes, of course." She swallowed nervously. "Where is your room?"

He nodded toward the carved wooden headboard. "On the other side of that wall. However, as you can see, there is no connecting door. No doubt you could get the desk clerk to supply you with a signed note to the effect that you spent the night alone if you're worried Paul will think we stayed together. Though I'll be damned if I can understand why you care what someone like Paul thinks." A hard ridge of muscle tightened along his jawline as he clenched his teeth.

"And I don't understand why, once I explained that the situation had changed, you deliberately antagonized Paul, humiliated me—"

"I don't consider it 'humiliating' to make it plain I think a woman is attractive and desirable."

Jan caught her breath, his unexpected comment triggering flashes of conflict within her. By now they were both inside the room, and with an angry, impatient shove, he sent the door spinning shut.

"Don't do that!" Jan gasped.

If he noticed the panic in her voice, he ignored it. "You aren't using good sense," he growled. "Paul Callison is a pompous snob with a computer for a heart. You should have said 'good riddance' when he dumped you and been thankful you didn't wind up married to him. Some other woman has evidently learned *her* lesson about marriage to him."

Jan dropped her purse on a chair. From what Paul said, she had assumed that he was the one who wanted the divorce. But that wasn't necessarily so. Well, what did it matter? "I think what is important is that Paul has recognized that he was wrong."

"He's done no such thing! He hasn't changed. He hasn't decided his snobbish, cold-blooded standards were wrong. He's just decided that maybe you meet those narrow-minded, prejudiced standards now."

"You're shouting. And I'd prefer that you go now." Jan turned her back on him and busied herself removing the gold earrings.

"Not until I talk some sense into you." He grabbed her shoulder and jerked her around to face him. "What did Paul ever say to you about love?"

"Love?" Jan repeated blankly. She held herself rigid against the harsh grip on her shoulder.

"Love. When Paul dumped you, did he say he was desperately in love with this other woman?"

"I—I don't remember."

Logan's voice softened a notch. "Jan, if he really fell deeply in love with the other woman, what he did to you might be understandable. Not necessarily fair, but understandable. Sometimes love just happens, and you can't do anything about it even if it isn't fair or appropriate. But if he made the cold-blooded decision that she would simply suit his corporate ambitions better..."

"I don't know..." Jan hadn't looked at it quite that way, and she found the idea disturbing. What had Paul's feelings for Corrinne been? "I'll have to talk to him."

Logan released her and paced across the large room as if it were too small to contain his anger. He whirled, as lithe on his feet as an acrobat. "Do you think he's interested in you now because he loves *you?*"

Jan walked around the bed, putting it protectively between herself and his anger. She was half-frightened of him, although she was determined not to show it. "No, of course not," she said carefully. "We haven't seen each other for six years."

"Real love doesn't end in six years. Or sixty. Paul Callison is too wrapped up in himself to love anyone. He has ice water in his veins. And if you're foolish enough to get involved with him again, you're going to get hurt again." He hesitated before adding reluctantly, "Maybe not right away. He'll marry you this time. You meet his computer printout standards now. But some things are a hell of a lot more painful than being dumped, and one of them is being married to the wrong person."

His outburst hit her with violent force, and she wavered under the onslaught. He could be right...

And he could be wrong, she reminded herself firmly. If Paul had changed his opinion about her, he could have changed in other ways, too. And he never had been all bad, just ambitious. She couldn't have fallen in love with him if he had been all-bad. She tried to remember what she had loved. He was brilliant and witty, hardworking, respected by others. Logan had never known Paul the way she had. And merely seeing and talking to Paul for one day was hardly getting "involved" with him, as Logan was suggesting.

"What are you doing?" Logan snapped sarcastically. "Remembering his talents as a lover?"

"No!" She should never have told him *everything!*

"You *don't* remember his talents as a lover? Perhaps that should tell you something," he mocked insinuatingly. A suddenly dangerous glint shone in his eyes. "I doubt you'd be so quick to forget if *I*..."

Jan glanced around nervously. She had already retreated as far as she could, and she berated herself for ever letting him get between her and the door. She drew herself up and tried to keep her voice calm. "Mr. Pierce, I have absolutely no interest in hearing about your expertise or exploits as a lover. And I didn't hire you for your advice. If you would please just *go* now..."

Anger flashed across his ruggedly handsome features, then vanished into something even more dangerous. He moved across the room toward her, eyes locked into hers, his steps silent on the carpet. She moistened her lips, wanting to scream or protest or run, but held in the magnetic grip of those eyes, craters of bottomless blue. He seemed to glide, a golden-hued predator with a mouth twisted into a taunting smile...or smiling snarl... He stopped scant inches away from her.

"That's right. You didn't hire me for my advice," he agreed, his voice soft but with a steel dagger hidden in it. He unsheathed the verbal dagger. "Just my body."

"You—you're being melodramatic," she faltered.

"Am I?"

Jan was tautly aware of the force and strength of that powerfully masculine body almost touching hers. His smile had a reckless glitter. She felt defenseless and vulnerable, helpless in some way that went beyond physical strength.

There was a dominating male force in him that made her feel submissive and yielding without his ever touching her. Submissive, yet with a strange, unfocused, tumultuous yearning inside her.

She turned, edging away from him, but the bed made an unyielding barrier against the back of her legs. The plush bedspread felt lush and sensuously inviting against her fingertips. She jerked her hands into a protective knot in front of her and summoned a scornful bravado. "I suppose this is where your paid dates usually end up, isn't it?" She stood her ground, fighting an urge to scramble across the bed in panicky retreat. "In the bed of some cheap motel. Paul may have his faults, but at least he doesn't—"

She broke off, suddenly afraid she had gone too far, but Logan finished the scornful sentence for her.

"At least he doesn't make love for money. Is that what you mean?" He smiled, not pleasantly.

"If you want to put it that crudely—yes! That's exactly what I mean."

A strange expression flickered across his face. "Perhaps the best thing that could happen to you would be if I *did* make love to you tonight."

"How dare you!" Jan gasped. In a pure, furious reflex action her hand flashed toward his face with deadly intent. But before she could slash a stinging blow across his cheek, he caught her wrist in the fast, powerful grip with which she was already too familiar.

They struggled silently for a moment until his greater strength and weight forced her backward across the bed. They landed with his body half over hers, his weight a crushing, smothering bulk that he made no effort to lift. He tangled one hand in her hair, and his mouth covered hers in a deep, bruising kiss that was more punishment than caress. His tongue probed her mouth arrogantly, and his hand slid beneath her disarranged blouse and closed roughly over the curve of her breast.

She felt the quickened thud of his heartbeat and the hard rush of aroused male passion in his body, but it was a harsh, angry passion without warmth or tenderness.

"Do you think you'll be so quick to forget this?" he asked with soft menace.

"I'm going to try!"

"You'll remember," he murmured with assurance just before his mouth covered hers again.

She felt only disgust for the physical force he used against her, but against her will something primitive and basic within her responded to the harsh caresses. A sensitivity leaped to life, as if a current had flashed through her, exposing exquisitely alive nerve ends. She felt the sensuous strength of his lips as his mouth mastered hers, and a sharp ache of desire tingled in her breasts. A harsh knee nudged her legs apart, and she felt the sinewy muscles of his legs against her thighs, bared as her skirt tangled around her hips in the fall. His lips moved down to conquer her throat after forcing her mouth into submissiveness. She closed her eyes, willing herself to remain rigid and unresponsive. Outwardly she succeeded. No muscle moved. No quiver betrayed her. But inwardly wildfire raged, lit by his burning kisses and the hot brand of his hand, a fire leaping from one vulnerable point to another within her. His hand found its way beneath the silken wisp of her bra and tightened until she almost cried out...though not in pain. Yes, it was pain, she thought wildly, the pain of longing, the feeling that she wanted to open herself to him and soar higher and higher...

His mouth dipped lower, from her throat to the swelling curve of her breast. And, instead of fighting him, she felt herself straining to bring the full yearning peak of her breast within reach of his lips. And then there was a small ripping sound as a button gave way under the relentless pressure of his advance.

The sound barely penetrated Jan's consciousness. Her mind was spinning through endless reaches of space that whirled somewhere inside her. And then she felt him go tense. The exquisite plunder of his mouth stopped. She opened her eyes and looked into his, staring down at her.

There was a strange, stunned look on his face, almost

an expression of wonder or disbelief, like a man seeing something awe-inspiring he had never seen before. He shifted his weight, not removing the hard contours of his body from their intimate fit against her yielding softness, but changing the pressure so she could breathe more freely again. Except that somewhere she had lost awareness of the harsh crush and welcomed the feel of his solid weight. The rough hand on her breast softened to a sensual caress and then moved away to smooth her blouse and then cover the vulnerably exposed curves.

"I've torn your blouse." He sounded remorseful.

"I can mend it."

A lock of hair, antique gold in the lamplight, fell across his forehead, but he didn't seem to notice. Instead he gently twisted a tendril of her hair around his finger and tucked it behind her ear.

"Logan . . . ?" Her voice made a question of his name, but she hardly knew what she asked. The wild desire within her that demanded instant satisfaction was gone, but in its place was a yearning ache that was deeper and sweeter and infinitely more precious . . . and confusing. It was in him, too. The desire was still there, but it was no longer an urge to punish or a demand for immediate selfish gratification. It was a desire to give as well as receive.

Jan felt as if something strange and singular had occurred. The revelation of a passion between them that was shocking in its power? Or the awakening of something even stronger that had brought the rushing, heedless passion to a halt? What had started in fury had changed to something else, and she had the strange feeling that he was as shaken by it as she was.

Logan rolled away from her abruptly, disentangling his legs from her skirt. She straightened the nubby, brown-gold silk self-consciously, aware of the exposed length of her thighs in sheer pantyhose.

"I'll see you in the morning?" She heard her own voice as if someone else were speaking, someone far more composed than she felt.

His gaze raked over her as he stood up. The brittle anger

was gone now. So was the passion. In their place was something enigmatic and unreadable.

"Maybe," he muttered thickly.

And then he was gone.

CHAPTER
Four

JAN SLID NAKED between the cool sheets. Her total nakedness did not expose a great deal more skin than the brief
nightie she usually wore, but the small difference was dis-
turbingly sensual. Her skin felt silky-smooth and ultrasen-
sitive, and she turned on her side to avoid the feel of the
upper sheet brushing her naked breasts. The uneasy thought
occurred to her that their particular sensitivity came not so
much from nakedness as from a lingering memory of Logan's touch. The touch that had changed from harsh anger
to velvet caress... She tossed restlessly, disturbed by the
lush vividness of that touch imprinted on her body. She
didn't want to remember it, as he had arrogantly assured
her she would remember.

A thump from the adjoining room tensed her into a sudden realization that Logan was sleeping only inches away

from her on the other side of the wall. Or *not* sleeping, she concluded from the sound of another muffled thump.

Another disturbing image assaulted her. Logan, not as she had always seen him, coolly sophisticated in a dinner jacket and black tie, but primitively naked, his hard-muscled body bronze against white sheets, a welcoming flash of smile on his face . . .

Now where had that particular thought come from, she wondered, aghast at the general direction her train of thought was taking. The pillow suddenly felt too warm, and she impatiently flopped it over to the other side, searching for a cool spot that would lull her into sleep. There was no reason she shouldn't sleep. The bed was large and comfortable. She had showered, rinsed out her pantyhose and underthings, mended the tiny rip using thread and a needle from a small sewing kit the motel provided and replaced the button on her blouse. Perhaps she was awake simply because she was hungry, she decided, feeling a distinctly empty rumble in her stomach.

But she knew it was more than that. This morning, when she had wakened in her bed in the Ventura apartment, seemed an eon ago. Another life. Why? Because she had learned Paul was free again, free and eager to rectify a mistake he had made six years ago? Or had the restless feeling of disorientation more to do with what had happened in this room with Logan tonight? Or what *hadn't* happened?

The turmoil of her thoughts churned on, but general exhaustion finally overcame her and she slept. When she woke, it was with the instant realization that she had overslept and it was late. Sheets and bedspread were tangled in disarray, and she had the vague, uncomfortable memory of having experienced some extremely erotic dream in the night, a dream that had taken her mental image of Logan lying naked and smiling in the bed several explicit steps further . . .

A sudden thought made her fling the tangled bedcovers aside and dash to the window.

The white Ferrari was gone.

She let the heavy drape drop back into place, feeling an

unexpected plunge of disappointment. So he really had decided to leave her here, as he had more or less implied he might last night.

Well, that was what she wanted, she reminded herself. Logan's earlier insistence on remaining here overnight if she did was quite ridiculous. Last night suddenly took on a kind of unreality, as if it were all part of that tantalizing dream-fantasy. Had she really felt that wild blaze of passion as she lay crushed beneath him on the bed? What, she wondered shakily, would have happened if he hadn't abruptly rolled away from her and stalked out? Would she have come to her senses in time?

She suddenly felt a little foolish, standing there stark naked in an unfamiliar motel room, asking herself unanswerable questions. Briskly, to dispel a lingering disappointment, she draped a towel sarong-style around her breasts and telephoned Paul at his mother's house. He said he would be over immediately to take her to breakfast. He asked cautiously about Logan and seemed relieved when Jan said Logan had gone back to Ventura.

She quickly applied a light makeup from the cosmetics kit she kept in her purse, dressed, and was just running a comb through her hair when she heard a car pull up outside. Paul really was eager to see her, she thought, gratified by his promptness. She unlatched the night lock and swung the door open.

"Logan!"

"Who were you expecting? The Avon lady?" He breezed through the door uninvited, bringing with him a brisk, outdoorsy scent and the tantalizing aroma of fresh pastry from a white box he was carrying. He was wearing faded jeans, jogging shoes, and a disreputable-looking gray sweatshirt with a hole in one sleeve. And he looked marvelous. Not stylishly debonair, as he had last night, but rested and casually windswept and cheerful, with a kind of pure animal vigor and vitality.

"What are you doing here?" she demanded. "I thought you'd gone back to Ventura."

"What made you think that?" He paused lightly in the

middle of the room. A maid pushing a linen cart passed by outside, and reluctantly Jan closed the door to her curious glance.

"Well, last night you sounded as if you might decide to leave. And then when I woke up your car was gone."

"I went to get some rolls and juice for breakfast. I thought you must be starved by now." He set the delectably fragrant bakery box on the table by the enameled hotplate. "Do you know how to make coffee in this thing?" he asked, picking up the Pyrex carafe.

"It's instant. You just have to heat the water."

Now, why had she said that? she wondered in angry agitation as she watched him fill the carafe breezily and set it on to heat. Why hadn't she told him that Paul would be here at any moment to take her to breakfast?

Instead she said, "Where did you get the clothes?"

"Fortunately, they happened to be left in the car from the last time I went sailing. Sorry I don't have an extra outfit for you." He opened the bakery box, and Jan's mouth and stomach reacted with healthy hunger. A frosted cinnamon roll looked almost maddeningly delicious.

Jan took a deep breath. "Really, I can't—"

"Sure you can. With your figure, you can afford to splurge on a couple of calorie-laden rolls just once." He ran an audacious glance up and down her slim but curvy figure. "Glass of orange juice first?"

"No." But when he thrust a styrofoam cup of juice at her, she accepted it helplessly. And just as helplessly found herself returning his brash grin. Why was Logan behaving this way this morning? He had a buoyant verve that made the slightly stale motel air crackle with charged energy. She half-regretted that she had been so hasty in telephoning Paul and agreeing to have breakfast with him.

"What this place needs is a little light." Logan marched over to the window and threw open the drapes. When he turned around, he seemed to see the tangled bed for the first time. "Well, well, what's this? Looks as if you spent a restless night."

"I heard you thumping around as if you didn't sleep any

too soundly yourself," Jan retorted.

"I suspect we'd both have spent a considerably more enjoyable night if we had shared one bed." Logan's eyes sparkled wickedly. "Though not necessarily *sleeping* any more than we did with a wall separating us. I kept thinking of you over here all alone, without so much as a nightgown to keep you warm . . ." He tilted his head in mock concern. His grin was pure deviltry.

Jan smothered a gasp at the boldly suggestive statements, but she wouldn't allow him to get the best of her and send her into some girlish twitter of embarrassment, though she already felt an incriminating flush of color rise to her cheeks. "I seem to recall that *you* were the one who stalked out," she pointed out recklessly.

"An impulsive action I regret thoroughly." He circled the bed and walked up to her. She folded her arms and held the cup of juice like a protective talisman in front of her. A talisman that was no protection at all, she realized, as he simply took the cup from her hand and set it aside. His fingertips traced a sensual pattern up her arms and locked beneath the thick curtain of hair at the nape of her neck. His eyes looked into hers for one long, heart-stopping moment, and then his mouth teased the corner of her lips while she held herself rigid, denying an almost overwhelming urge to turn her mouth recklessly to his. "We could take up where we left off last night . . ."

Jan had thought she could afford to be bold with her taunting statement about his walking out last night. The night and its dangers were over. But he had turned the tables on her, met her challenge and called her bluff. And the dangers weren't over. She could feel them swirling through her, tantalizing her with heady desire. She tried to take a step backwards, but his locked hands slid down to her waist.

"It's broad daylight!" she protested wildly.

"If you make love only under cover of darkness, you're missing something very special." His voice was a silky invitation.

"No, that isn't what I meant! I meant—" She broke off, losing her train of thought as his powerful hands tilted her

hips toward his. She gulped a steadying breath and tried to
ignore the intimate contact. "I meant, I—I don't want to
make love with you at all! Not—not anytime."

"Don't you?"

He gave her a lazy, knowing smile, and in dismay she
realized that her arms had betrayed her, that somehow, of
their own volition, they had unfolded and slid around him.
She clenched her hands into fists, refusing to give into the
desire to run her palms in wild abandon over the smooth,
hard muscles of his back.

"Why did you stay here?" she asked.

"I had in mind seeing that you got home safely." He
kissed the tip of her nose.

"Paul said he'd drive me back to Ventura."

"I don't recall that Paul is exactly famous for his relia-
bility in looking after your welfare." He leaned back slightly
to look down into her eyes. "Stay away from him, Jan," he
said, his lightly teasing tone changing to sudden urgency.
"He—"

A knock on the door interrupted. Logan's glance flicked
to the door, then back to Jan.

"It's Paul. I called him a few minutes ago. He's taking
me to breakfast. Champagne brunch, actually. I—I'm
sorry," she faltered, and then she was angry at herself. She
had nothing to be sorry about. Yet, incongruously, she *was*
sorry. Logan's going out for juice and rolls was a sweet,
considerate gesture, and sharing rolls and instant coffee here
with him was strangely far more appealing than the most
elegant brunch with Paul.

But she didn't *want* Logan doing sweet, considerate
things for her. It was too confusing, too unsettling.

Logan lifted his eyebrows. "Champagne brunch. I see.
I should have known my concern for your—ummm—lack
of nourishment was misplaced. Obviously you're the type
who always manages to look out for herself." His voice was
sardonic, but still he didn't release her, and the knock
sounded again.

"If you'll figure out what I owe you, I'll send you a
check," Jan said hurriedly. "I wasn't planning on a motel

bill, and I didn't bring enough cash."

Abruptly Logan released her. She staggered a little, not realizing how strongly his arms had been supporting her. The water in the carafe was boiling furiously. Logan dumped it in the bathroom sink.

"You'd better answer the door."

Jan glanced nervously at the door, then back at Logan haphazardly scooping rolls into the bakery box. "About your fee—"

"Forget it!" he snapped. He squashed the lid down on the carton in a savage movement. "I think I'll chalk this one up to experience."

He flung the door open and strode past an astonished-looking Paul as if the other man didn't exist. Paul stepped inside, his gray eyes taking in the rumpled bed and Jan's flushed face. The fragrance of the pastries lingered in the air and lent an additional suspiciously cozy intimacy to the scene.

"Logan just stopped by for a minute to see if I wanted some breakfast rolls," Jan explained in a rush before Paul could get the wrong idea. "I told him I was having breakfast with you. His room is next door."

"I see." Paul's expression was frankly suspicious. "I thought you said he went back to Ventura last night."

"I thought he had, but it turned out he hadn't," Jan said lamely. Then she was suddenly annoyed with Paul for putting her on the defensive. She had done nothing wrong. It was Paul, after all, who had committed the real wrong, six years ago. She tossed her head and looked at Paul defiantly, stubbornly refusing to offer any further explanation.

"Are you ready to leave, then?" he asked finally, evidently deciding not to press the issue.

Jan made a quick tour through the bathroom to make sure she hadn't left anything. She flipped the covers on the bed surreptitiously as she passed it. It surely looked more rumpled than one person's sleeping alone could have made it. She winced as a sudden squeal of tires outside informed her that the Ferrari was leaving, with its owner obviously not in a particularly good humor.

It was not an auspicious beginning, but the tense air between Paul and Jan relaxed gradually over the leisurely champagne brunch. Paul couldn't seem to get enough of looking at her, and both his attentiveness and compliments were flattering and gratifying. He complimented her hair, figure, clothing, even obliquely acknowledged being grudgingly impressed with her relationship with a man of Logan Pierce's caliber. He was full of plans about things they could do together.

Jan listened and smiled and nodded at appropriate places. This was the moment for which, six years ago, she would have sold her soul. But now, much to her annoyance, she kept seeing Paul with Logan's jaundiced eye. She kept peering around behind the compliments and plans, searching for the *real* Paul Callison. Had he changed? Jan was uncertain. He seemed unnecessarily curt with the waitress, overly picky about his food. Yet those were minor defects, and the waitress *was* slow. Jan cautiously tried to get Paul to talk about his ex-wife and his early feelings about her, but all she got were some bitter comments about Corrinne's failure to live up to her responsibilities. Responsibilities, Jan gathered slowly, that had more to do with her position as a corporate executive's wife than with love.

Jan tried to shake a mocking I-told-you-so image of Logan from her mind, but it stubbornly refused to go away. It watched her at every turn, cynically questioned every statement Paul made, and snapped wickedly irreverent comments about Paul's most profound observations.

"Are you feeling all right?" Paul asked suddenly.

"Yes. Of course." She had no idea what he had just been talking about. She floundered for something suitable to add to the conversation. "This Canadian bacon is delicious."

"You seem a little distracted."

She *was* distracted, she realized in annoyance. Distracted by Logan's supicions about Paul. Equally distracted by disturbing thoughts about Logan himself. Wondering if he really had gone back to Ventura. Remembering that heady male vitality about him and her own electrified reaction. Frowning at his arrogant advice-giving. Thinking, with a strange little twinge of regret that confused her, that she would probably never see him again.

Jan glanced at Paul, a speculative thought crossing her mind. He knew about her past travel-and-television job with Adele Meeker, and also that she had moved to Ventura to take a television job. Would his attitude toward her change if he knew she didn't presently have some glamour position, that she was, in fact, quite unemployed?

She spread it all out for him bluntly—the station manager's death, her unsatisfactory interview with Bruce Gurley, the disadvantage of not having a university degree. She realized it was something of a test, and she waited for Paul's reaction with interest but also a certain detachment.

He frowned slightly. "Cindy gave me the impression you'd gone to college after all."

"Night classes. I never got near a degree."

"I see." She could feel the computer chips clicking in his mind. That little mocking figure of Logan inside her own head taunted, "Aha! See? Now you *don't* measure up to his snobbish standards." But Paul just shrugged. "A college education is no big deal. Just say you have a degree. No one will ever check. Just make it some relatively obscure, out-of-state university so you won't get trapped by someone who actually went to the place you name."

Jan's eyes widened. "That sounds a little—underhanded."

Paul leaned across the table and took her hand in his. "Jan, you're more intelligent and cultured and talented and beautiful than any college girl I ever met," he said earnestly. With a grimace he added, "Including my ex-wife."

Jan was left undecided as to whether or not Paul had passed her little test.

The drive back to Ventura in Paul's big luxury Buick was pleasant. Once Jan caught herself nodding off to sleep, but she quickly attributed that to a lack of rest last night than boredom with Paul's talk about his company. They also talked of places to which they had both traveled, music, movies, plays. Jan knew Paul was going to ask to see her again, but even as the car glided to a stop in front of her apartment, she still was undecided as to how she was going to respond. Her feelings were definitely mixed.

Paul's lavish compliments and rekindled interest in her were gratifying. He had made every effort to be charming today. She had not a shred of doubt that, if she continued to see him, he would very soon ask her to marry him.

But had she really any interest in marrying him? She had to face the possibility that there was a none-too-admirable part of her that would like a proposal from him simply to satisfy her bruised ego, damaged when he dumped her six years ago. And perhaps seek a bit of nasty vengeance when she informed him tartly that he didn't meet *her* standards now?

Jan's thoughts were further confused by a vague feeling that she might be letting Logan's acid comments and suspicions about Paul unfairly color her attitude toward him. But if she agreed to see Paul again, would she be doing it because she really wanted to see him, or because of a certain stubborn refusal to let Logan Pierce dictate arrogantly to her? And there was the additional complication of her turbulent feelings about Logan himself...

In the end, she agreed to see Paul the following weekend, mostly because she felt she needed to investigate and explore her own unsettled feelings further. She was out of the car and in the apartment before she realized that she had unconsciously, but quite deftly, managed to avoid the goodbye kiss Paul had wanted to give her.

Jan retrieved her car just before dark, relieved to find it intact and undamaged. The thought had rather tardily occurred to her that leaving it overnight in the shopping center parking lot wasn't the smartest thing to do. Later she gave Shelley a somewhat edited version of the wedding weekend, carefully deleting all mention of Logan.

She only wished, Jan thought unhappily, that she could as easily delete him from her thoughts. His assurance that she wouldn't be able to forget his embrace rankled, but she had to admit unhappily that he was right.

On Monday she drove out to Ojai again, but the receptionist at the television station told her that everyone was tied up in conferences all week. The girl was friendly, confiding that the station was really in an uproar since Mr. Anderson's death, but perhaps everything would be back to normal by next week. Jan contemplated looking for another job, but decided that it wouldn't be fair to take something and then quit abruptly if a position at the television station opened up. She could hold out a little longer, she decided, eyeing her checkbook Monday evening.

Looking at the checkbook reminded her of something else that was nagging at her. She hadn't paid Logan. He had caustically stated that he planned to "chalk this one up to experience," but the more she thought about it, the more determined she was not to accept any favors from *him*. She owed the money and she would pay it.

Her mind made up, Jan waited impatiently for Shelley to go out somewhere with her fiancé, as she usually did, so Jan could call Logan. In frustration, Jan saw Shelley settle into a cross-legged positon on the sofa with the announcement that she was going to spend the evening changing the hemlines on a couple of dresses she planned to take along on a weekend visit with her fiancé's parents.

Concealing a sigh, Jan decided to postpone the telephone call until the following evening. But after fifteen minutes of fidgeting and staring at the same magazine page, she abruptly mumbled something vague to Shelley about going for a drive. She drove directly to the phone booth outside the drugstore at the shopping center. She refused to speculate on the possibility that her impatience with any delay in calling Logan came because she was inordinately eager to hear his voice. She merely wanted to resolve this awkward and unfinished situation, she assured herself.

She didn't have to look up the number. Somehow it was already branded on her mind. The phone was picked up on the second ring.

"Hello." The snapped word sounded as if he weren't in a particularly good humor.

"Hi. This is Jan. Jan McFarland?" Her voice ended on a peculiar, questioning upswing, as if she weren't certain he would remember her.

There was a moment of silence, then his sardonic, "You did get back to Ventura safely, I take it."

"Yes, of course. I—I just called about paying your fee."

"I told you to forget it. The experience was"—he paused and then finished with a certain sour amusement— "invaluable. And enlightening.'"

"No, I insist on paying you." A truck rumbled by on the street, and Jan had to cover one ear with her hand to shut out the noise. "We had an agreement. One hundred dollars, plus the cost of a meal, and the motel rooms."

"I'm sure you can add it up as well as I can." He sounded half-angry now.

"Very well. If you'll give me an address to which to send the check?"

There was a noisy *clunk* as if he had just knocked something over, or slammed his fist against a desk in annoyance. "Jan, this is ridic—" He broke off in mid-word, the silence so abrupt that for a moment Jan thought they had been disconnected. "I'll pick it up in person. We'll have dinner, and you can tell me all about your conquest of Paul."

Jan hesitated, torn between a previously unacknowledged desire to see him again, and a reluctance to have him come to the apartment where Shelley might see and recognize him.

Logan misinterpreted the delay. "Or does Paul already have you booked up seven nights a week?"

"Of course not!"

"But you are seeing him again," Logan pursued.

"Yes. Saturday evening." Suddenly Jan remembered that Shelley and her fiancé were leaving right after work Friday for the weekend visit with his parents. "But I could give you the check Friday night."

"Fine." He asked for her address and she gave it to him. Before he hung up, he made another unexpected request. "Bring along a snapshot of yourself before this big transformation took place, okay? I'd like to see just what Paul rejected the first time around."

The request caught Jan totally by surprise, but she stammered a qualified assent, saying she would bring one if she still had any old photos around after having moved and traveled so much.

Tuesday, Wednesday, and Thursday limped along. Jan kept busy studying the Ojai station's programming and style, and working on ideas for her own show, but she felt restless and distracted. Finally she had to admit that she was as impatient for Friday evening to arrive as a six-year-old waiting for a birthday. She had no idea how the evening would turn out. She already knew Logan could be sensitive and understanding . . . and exciting. He could just as easily be caustic and disagreeable. One thing he would never be, she realized with a certain mixture of anticipation and apprehension, was dull.

Paul called Thursday evening. He suggested that she drive into Los Angeles Saturday evening so they could attend an informal swim and barbecue party with some friends from his company. Jan wasn't wild about the idea of driving into L. A. through heavy weekend traffic, but it was just as inconvenient for him to drive out to Ventura, she reminded herself, and finally she agreed.

Jan breathed a sigh of relief when Shelley dashed in after work on Friday, changed clothes, and grabbed her suitcase. Now there definitely would be no awkward complications or embarrassment when Logan arrived. She had plenty of time to luxuriate in a hot tub of bubbles. Logan hadn't indicated where they were going for dinner, and she hesitated in front of her closet after the leisurely bath. She didn't want to dress as if she considered the dinner an important occasion, but neither did she want to look scruffy. Finally she chose all-occasion dressy black evening pants, classic vanilla blouse, and medium-heeled sandals. She brushed her hair into the usual tousle of casual curls swinging around her shoulders.

When the doorbell rang, she paused for a last-minute check in the mirror and saw a dancing, dark brilliance in her eyes. A something-wonderful-is-going-to-happen look, she thought a little breathlessly.

Something did happen when she opened the door. But

not something wonderful, even though she saw a blue-diamond glitter of masculine interest in Logan's appraising eyes as he stepped inside.

"Well, you're looking unusually sparkly tonight." He added caustically, "Something to do with Paul, no doubt?"

Jan's breathless feeling of anticipation collapsed like the ratings on a bad television show. "I really don't care to discuss Paul any further."

"You prefer just to jump headlong into a mistake."

Three days of anticipation wasted, Jan thought, because less than sixty seconds into seeing Logan she was already seething with anger at his arrogance.

"I really don't think there's any point in our going to dinner." Jan deliberately put a frosty edge on her voice. "I'll just give you your money now." She fished the check out of her purse and thrust it at him.

He stuffed it in his jacket pocket without looking at it, but made no move to go. He was wearing a well-cut dark blue suit—nothing exceptional at all about it, or about the white shirt and discreet wine-colored tie. Yet there was nothing even remotely ordinary-looking about him. His presence dominated the small living room. It would have even if he weren't almost indecently handsome, Jan realized with surprise.

"I suppose I could promise not to mention Paul again," he offered, none too graciously.

"I suppose I have to eat," she agreed, just as ungraciously.

His chiseled lips twitched, and she felt the pull of a giggle tickling the corners of her mouth. Then they both broke out laughing.

"What happened to the usual routine of small talk at the beginning of a date?" Jan asked accusingly. "Things like, *hi, there. What a pretty blouse. Your hair looks lovely.*"

"I suppose I did come on like the outraged father, suspicious that every guy is out to seduce his beautiful daughter," Logan admitted. "It's just that I can see right through Paul, and I know he hasn't changed, and you're going to get hurt again if—" At the warning tilt of Jan's head, he broke off and reached for her hands. "Okay. I promise. No more Father-knows-best advice. How about, hi, there! What a lovely blouse. Your hair looks gorgeous."

Jan ignored the "compliments." "What difference does it make to you if I get hurt?" she asked slowly.

He looked uncharacteristically bemused. "I'll be damned if I know," he muttered. The small, perplexed frown passed, and he grinned again. "But you do look gorgeous. Really." His lips brushed her cheek lightly.

They went to dinner at a restaurant situated atop a hotel near the ocean. Their window table gave them a view of jeweled city lights against a backdrop of rolling, darkly mysterious mountain silhouettes. They ordered steaks and talked of little things—impersonal things, really—yet an undercurrent of excitement flowed between them, making the most mundane of subjects exhilarating. Logan kept looking at her eyes, and their radiance seemed to lend a starry sparkle to everything she viewed. The wine in her glass was a ruby jewel, Logan's eyes brilliant midnight-blue, the candle an iridescent flame. Once he touched her hand across the table, and the contact sent tongues of fire flickering up her arm, all out of proportion to a mere meeting of fingertips. Their eyes met again and something leaped between them, the contact so dazzling that Jan had to look away.

And then she noticed something else. The mountain silhouettes and jeweled lights had disappeared, and a dark gulf lay beyond the window, broken only by a scattered twinkling of lights. Logan noted her astonishment.

"The dining room rotates," he explained. "We're looking out over the ocean now. I thought you might enjoy the changing view."

Jan had had no sensation of movement before, but now she thought she felt it, subtle and powerful beneath her feet. Logan smiled, enjoying her surprise and pleasure. And with the change from civilized city to moon-drenched ocean scene came another subtle change. Jan was still aware of the radiant glitter that seemed to surround them, but she was also aware of other things much more basic and earthy—the sensuous curve of Logan's mouth as he laughed, the latent strength in his hand as he touched hers lightly, the husky timbre of his voice that sometimes seemed to caress her even as he spoke of casual matters. He had selected their meal carefully, chosen the wine with discriminating good taste, but he ate heartily, with obvious enjoyment and none of Paul's picky fussiness. Somewhere in the back of Jan's mind lurked the seductive thought that perhaps this indicated something else basic and earthy and sensual about him . . .

A brisk breeze was blowing when they went back out to the Ferrari, and Logan cupped her elbow with a lightly protective gesture. "Would you mind if we drove over to the marina for a few minutes?" he asked. "I've been having some problems with the auxiliary engine on my sailboat, and a mechanic was supposed to be out to work on it. I'd like to check and see if he came."

Jan had no objections. When they reached the marina, Logan opened the car door and said he'd be just a minute.

"May I come, too?" Jan asked impulsively. "I'd like to see your sailboat."

"The wind is really blowing here," he warned. "Your hair will get mussed."

"I don't mind if you don't."

Two steps out of the car and Jan knew what he meant. Her hair was more than "mussed." The wind whipped it around her face and throat with whirling-dervish abandon. It was in her eyes and mouth until she managed to gather it into a sideswept, hand-held ponytail. Logan grabbed her other hand and, leaning slightly against the wind, they made their way out to the boat slip his sailboat occupied.

A platinum moon soared overhead. A wisp of cloud scudding across the moon's face gave the illusion that the clouds were standing still and the moon moving, sailing in regal splendor across an obstacle-ridden sky. The marina was a forest of sailboat masts of varying heights. In the hard wind, taut ropes banging against masts made a clashing crescendo of sound that was strangely melodic, with a counterpoint of unidentifiable tinkles and bongs and clangs.

Jan listened entranced, unmindful of the cold wind assaulting her hair or biting through her open jacket. It was like music from another world or time, hinting at adventure on the high seas or mysterious and forbidden loves in secret Oriental palaces, where the clash of cymbals might mean death or ecstasy. They stopped at the sleek bow of the small craft. Logan braced her, both hands gripping her arms while she caught her breath against the wind.

"Most girls don't smile when their hairdos are being ripped to shreds by the wind."

"Am I smiling?" But she knew she was. The moon, the wild caress of the wind, the musical clang, all exhilarated her, made her feel as if she might soar with the racing moon.

"I'll unlock the cabin, and you can wait inside while I check the engine."

He bridged the gap of dark water between concrete dock and boat with a lithe leap and held out a hand to guide Jan while she followed. He stepped down ahead of her into the shadowy lower level of the cockpit, and she balanced on the narrow walkway around it. Beneath her, the boat rolled slightly with the gentle movement of the water.

"Do you ever sail at night?"

"I have. But not tonight. It's calm here, but the open water is too rough tonight for a boat this size. The channel can be dangerous."

As if to prove that even this protected area wasn't totally safe, a sudden lurch of the deck plunged Jan into the cockpit. Logan caught her as she tumbled forward, breaking her fall with his body and arms. Her hands clutched him instinctively as her body collided with his, her face smothered in the broad width of his chest. When she straightened up, her arms went around him.

The boat rocked gently beneath their feet, moving their molded bodies in unison to a primeval rhythm. In the moonlight, Logan's sculptured features appeared strangely brooding as he looked down into her upturned face. His arms held her so tightly that her ribs ached, and she felt light-headed as her lips parted in breathless anticipation for his kiss. But the kiss didn't come. He just kept looking at her, that strange, brooding expression on his face. His legs were spread and braced for balance, and she could feel the tensed muscles of his thighs moving against her legs with the jolting rhythm of the boat.

Jan raised herself recklessly on tiptoe and strained toward him. She had never in her life wanted to be kissed more than she did at this moment. She ached for it, an ache that seemed to be spreading all through her straining body.

His head dipped and Jan's eyes drifted shut, though the moonlight was so bright that it was an almost physical touch on her closed eyelids. And then there was another touch on her eyelids, kisses so feathery-light that they felt like an extension of the moonlight caress.

Jan stood there, pressing her body against his, her face upturned to the delicate shower of kisses on her eyes and temples and the vulnerable curve of her throat. At last she felt the tender rain change to a hard, hungry exploration of her mouth. His hands moved down to hold her hips captive against the hard contours of his body.

And then he thrust her roughly away, through the door of the small cabin. "Get inside. You're shaking with the cold. I'll check the engine."

But it wasn't the cold that was making her tremble, she protested silently. It was him.

He followed her inside the cabin long enough to turn on a light over a small sink. His head nearly touched the low ceiling. The light bulb had an uncertain yellowish glow.

"Battery must be getting weak," he muttered.

He removed his jacket, tossed it across the bed, and rolled up his shirt sleeves. In the faint glow of the light the fine hair on his forearms had a metallic golden glint. He found a flashlight and wrench in a drawer and disappeared outside.

Jan smoothed her disheveled hair, then folded her arms and tucked her hands inside the sleeves of her jacket. The cabin shut out the cutting wind, but the small room was still distinctly cool. From outside came a few clunks and thuds and a muttered oath as Logan did something with the engine.

Once the engine rumbled, then coughed and sputtered to a stop.

Jan peered around in the dim light. The cabin was tiny but efficiently compact with an alcohol stove, a tiny table that folded out from a wall, and a three-quarter-size bed with sleeping bag casually slung over it. A cupboard or drawer occupied every niche and corner to make use of every available inch of space. It was all neat and clean, yet it had an unmistakably bachelor air, with no feminine touches at all. Jan opened a cupboard and peered inside curiously. Canned chili, chicken-noodle soup, corned beef. Sturdy bachelor food. Another narrow cupboard held instant coffee and tea bags.

On sudden impulse Jan poked around until she found a small aluminum pan and matches to light the stove. A hand pump beside the tiny sink produced a pencil-sized stream of water from a storage tank somewhere on board.

The water was bubbling on the stove when the door burst open a few minutes later. A cold draft of damp air swept in, and with it a wind-lashed Logan, his dark gold hair tossed like a lion's mane. His hands were greasy, and he looked chilled and thoroughly disgusted.

"I think the mechanic fouled up the engine worse than it was already."

He washed his hands, dried them on a paper towel, and forced the burnt gold tangle of his hair into place with his fingers, not bothering to look in a mirror. Then he noted the boiling water and waiting cups. He arched an eyebrow. "What's this?"

"I thought you might like a cup of coffee to warm up."

Jan had been huddling over the small flame from the stove, trying to keep comfortable, and the cabin had warmed slightly, but it was Logan's virile presence that suddenly seemed to raise the temperature several degrees. Or was it, Jan wondered as she handed Logan a cup of coffee, just that his presence raised *her* temperature several steamy degrees? His muscular frame filled the compact room with masculine energy and vitality.

He looked at the coffee and then at Jan, apparently abandoning thoughts of the inept mechanic and engine problems. "I'm sure," he said with a dark, speculative gleam in his eyes, "that we could think of a better way to get warm."

CHAPTER
Five

JAN TOOK A half-step backward, all she could manage in the tiny confines of the cabin. She stared at him wide-eyed, a rush of indignation at the audacity of his insinuation grappling with opposing ripples of treacherous excitement. "I didn't come here to—"

"I was merely suggesting adding a bit of brandy to the coffee." His voice was smooth, and he flashed her an innocent smile, though his eyes had a less-innocent gleam.

He reached into another cubbyhole and brought out a slim bottle. After a moment's hesitation Jan held out her cup, and he trickled a little of the richly glowing liquid into the coffee. She had the feeling he was laughing at her, though his expression remained carefully composed. His hand was steady as he poured, but hers, holding the cup, had an incriminating tremble. Quickly, to hide it, she put the cup to her mouth and took a sip. The smooth coffee-brandy blend slid down her throat with a sweet, racing fire. Between the warming drink and the heat of the small flame on the stove . . . and the blood-stirring warmth of Logan's presence . . . Jan felt an unexpected flush steal through her. She fervently hoped it wasn't as obvious externally as it felt internally.

"Do you do a lot of sailing?" Jan asked quickly, to change the subject. She squeezed her hip against the narrow counter. In the small cabin she felt as if she almost had to hold her breath to keep from touching him.

"I sail whenever I can spare the time. It's relaxing. Perhaps you'd like to sail out to the Channel Islands sometime?" He threw his jacket aside and sat down on the edge of the bed.

"Are those the islands I can see from town?"

Logan nodded. "Five islands were only recently made into a national park. Lots of sea lions and seals, including some of the rather strange elephant seals, live on the islands. Anacapa is the island people usually visit."

"That sounds marvelous," Jan agreed enthusiastically. "I'd love to go."

"And I'd love to have you sit down here beside me and stop acting as if you're afraid we might set the sailboat on fire if we happen to touch each other accidentally."

A little stiffly, Jan perched primly on the edge of the bed and took tiny sips of the hot coffee. His comment had sounded amused, but it was all too accurate and did little to relieve the static electricity darting around inside her. Indeed, she felt as if something incendiary was hovering between them, ready for any spark to explode it out of control.

"It's a lovely boat. But I don't know anything about crewing or whatever it is passengers do on a sailboat." She made a valiant effort to keep her mind on sailing.

"I can handle the boat alone." In the yellowish light that seemed to be growing dimmer, Logan's face had changed to a thoughtful expression. "Did you bring along a picture?"

"Oh, yes!" Jan dug in her purse, making more of a flurry

of activity out of the hunt than was really necessary. "Two, actually. One is my high school graduation picture. The other is with my brother Mike, after his accident."

Logan inspected the photographs carefully, slanting them to catch the dim glow from the bulb. Jan studied them, too. She was a little surprised, looking at the girl in the photographs from the perspective of time, to see that she had been a little plump back then, but hardly "dumpy", as she always thought of herself.

She waited expectantly for some comment from Logan, but none was forthcoming. "What do you think?" she asked finally as he handed back the photographs.

"I promised not to mention Paul."

"What does that mean?" she asked, puzzled.

"It means I think he was a fool for not knowing what he had six years ago. And for not hanging onto it."

"You probably wouldn't have noticed me if we'd met six years ago," Jan retorted, "so you shouldn't blame Paul—"

"I'd have noticed," Logan interrupted without a trace of doubt. "And I'd have wanted to do just what I intend to do right now."

His eyes trapped and held hers as, with slow deliberateness, he removed the cup from her nerveless hands and set it on the counter. The boat rocked gently as his mouth moved inexorably toward hers. She felt as if she were caught within the vortex of some swirling force, subtle and more powerful than the force that rotated the restaurant in sweeping circles. Her head tilted to receive his kiss, moved by that same irresistible power. His mouth touched hers, not with the brief, explosive force of some quickly dissipated fireworks, but like an all-consuming river that swept her along in its relentless flow.

His mouth had the sweet-fiery taste of brandy, but it wasn't the liquor that sent a heady intoxication flowing through Jan. His virile power was more potent than any liquor, flowing around and through her, enveloping her in that molten river. She let her mouth simply receive the kiss, opened it to the exploring probe of his tongue, and reveled in the exploration with luxurious abandon.

When he finally lifted his head, Jan felt as if some vital element of her being had been separated from her. His head hovered over hers. She didn't know when it had happened, but she was lying back against the bed now. The down-filled sleeping bag pillowed her like a sensuous nest. Her fingertips traced the line of his jaw, exploring angular bone and taut skin. Skin smooth-shaven but with the ever-so-faint raspiness of whiskers, like some hidden male secret that hinted at deeper, more primitive secrets. Secrets she longed to explore...

"The light is going out." She spoke without taking her eyes from the hollowed shadows of his. The bulb was barely a yellow glow now, like a candle guttering out. The music of wind playing discords with ropes and masts was muted here in the cushion of downy softness, but it rose and fell with an unseen rhythm.

"I'll have to do something about that..." In an easy gesture, he reached up and flicked the light switch, his body returning to hers before her kiss-drugged mind could even think of moving away. He kissed her again, and she felt as if she were floating, though she dimly realized the weight-less feeling came because he lifted her with one powerful arm and slipped the jacket deftly from her shoulders.

Her eyes drifted open, finding the cabin a contrast be-tween inky shadow and a single oblong of silvery moonlight slanting through the lone window. The oblong spotlighted her from throat to waist. Almost as if she were seeing it happen to someone else, she watched his hands move from button to button of her cream-colored blouse. They were disembodied hands, for she could see nothing else of him in the shadowy cavern of the alcove that held the bed. When the last button fell free, he spread the silky material of the blouse to reveal the lace-covered, softly rounded mounds of her breasts. His mouth dipped to explore with unhurried leisure the swelling curves and moon-sculptured hollow between them, with occasional tantalizing nudges toward the lace-hidden peaks.

She should stop him, she thought. But it was an idle,

almost languid thought. There was plenty of time. He did everything with such a delicious, honeyed slowness. They were both savoring anticipation of the moment when he finally slipped his hands beneath her to remove the restraining barrier of lace. She felt as much as heard the small animal growl of pleasure in his throat as she lay naked from the waist up in the oblong of moonlight.

A small hint of alarm trembled through her. She suddenly felt vulnerably exposed in the silvery spotlight that seemed to make some pagan altar of her taut breasts, an altar that held Logan spellbound. She tried to move out of the light, but he held her motionless.

"Don't move," he whispered huskily. "I want to look at you." He looked and then he touched, first with fingertips as delicate as a whisper, then with his tongue in feathery caress, and finally with the full enveloping force of his mouth. Hungry surges swept through her, waves of longing thundering in an unleashed storm of passion.

Until then she had only received, absorbed the delicious pleasure he had to give, drank it in like a thirsty sponge. But now the waves of passion swept outward. She fumbled frantically with his shirt and tie, her eager hands as awkward as if she wore mittens, until he laughed unrestrainedly and flung shirt and tie aside in a glorious gesture of abandon. Now the oblong of moonlight gleamed on his naked chest.

"I like to look at you, too," she whispered. She ran her hands over muscles that gleamed metallically but felt warm and alive against her fingertips.

Moments later they were both naked on the bed together, side by side in the down-padded cocoon, and the joyous exploration continued. He found the long curve of her hip and the sensitive area just inside her hipbone, caressed the satin skin of her thighs and returned again and again to the soft roundness of her breasts. Her fingertips traced the swirl of fine hair on his abdomen and the lean, hard muscle underlying it.

His mouth offered a smorgasbord of delights to her willing body, a spicy touch of his lips here, a tantalizing appetizer of a caress there, a delicious confection of all-over kisses that exquisitely filled the small, giddy hungers of her body . . . only to arouse another deeper and more demanding hunger.

And when she thought she couldn't stand it any longer, when her body felt as exquisitely sensitive as some finely tuned instrument, he slid over her. They sank into each other as if they were entering into another world, and for a breathless, motionless moment became one with each other and the universe, timeless and eternal in the first intimate revelations of a self each gave and received.

Then, as if determined to bring them back to more earthy and less ethereal knowledge, the gentle rocking of the boat awakened them to the physical delights of their intimately molded bodies. For a few moments, they simply flowed with the fluid motion of the boat, letting their bodies sway to the delicately undulating rhythm that fused them together as one. Jan felt as if she could go on forever like this, drifting in a dreamy world of sensuously undulating movement, but then the softly rocking motion began to hint seductively of deeper and ever more satisfying pleasures. Her hips began a small, instinctive movement of their own, almost imperceptible at first, just the smallest hint of emphasis with each gentle roll of the boat. But Logan felt it and with a small growl of sudden impatience, his masculine forces took command, carrying them both to undreamed-of heights and holding them there with an inner power that went beyond the physical. Jan met him with shameless abandon and a feminine strength of her own, rising with him until the crashing crescendo within them mingled with the wildly discordant music of the wind outside.

Jan drifted back slowly, finding herself snuggled securely against the warm animal heat of Logan's body. His arms were around her, one side of the sleeping bag thrown partially over both of them. She had the strange feeling that something monumental had happened, that she had crossed some barrier far more elemental than the long-ago physical loss of innocence. She was a little shocked at herself. She wasn't the kind to fall so quickly into a physical relationship. Shocked . . . but too happy and satisfied to be sorry.

"Logan?" she asked tentatively.

He made some throaty sound in reply, wordless and satisfied, and kissed the curve of her temple. She snuggled closer and closed her eyes, her leg seeking the comfortable niche between his. She was almost asleep when he stirred slightly.

"Will you stay with me tonight?" he whispered against her hair.

"It looks as if I am," she murmured sleepily.

He raised up on one elbow. "Not here. At my place."

"Why?" She felt warm and comfortable, infinitely relaxed and secure, loath to move an inch, let alone get up out of the bed.

He laughed softly. "Look."

She raised up and looked. Clouds had drifted across the moon, and now the moonlight was a diffused glow instead of a sharp silver oblong. She saw his clothes carelessly dangling over the edge of the bed, half on the floor. Her evening slacks were a dark puddle on the floor, her silk blouse lost somewhere beneath her, her lacy bra a risqué ornament at the foot of the bed.

In the soft glow of moonlight, the disheveled scene of their reckless lovemaking had a certain careless charm, but Jan knew that in the cold gray light of morning it could all look a bit tawdry. Logan knew it, too, and she felt a quick rush of warmth and gratitude for his sensitivity, for his desire that what had happened between them not be cheapened by any hint of awkwardness or tawdriness.

"We'll go to my place and soak in the hot tub, and I'll bring you breakfast in bed." He spoke softly and curled a tendril of her hair around one finger and brushed her cheek with his lips. With laughter in his voice, he added, "And then I'll make you get up and hike through my avocado orchard and up in the hills with me."

"We'll have to stop by my apartment to pick up some clothes. I can hardly go hiking in high-heeled sandals."

"There are things I have to tell you," he said with a sudden, unexpected urgency. "Things I probably should have told you before this."

Jan shifted her weight to look at him, but she could see

only the dark, unrevealing shadow of his outline. "Something serious?" she asked lightly, a little disturbed by his intensity.

"Maybe." He kissed her nose. "But it can wait until tomorrow."

They dressed, bumping into each other, tangling arms and legs and clothes, giggling like a couple of adolescents at a slumber party. Logan drove quickly to her apartment. Jan was surprised to see a light on inside. She must have forgotten and left it on when she left. They were almost to the steps when the apartment door opened and Shelley came flying out.

Jan stopped short. "Shelley!" she gasped. "What are you doing here?"

"Jeff's car broke down before we even got to Santa Barbara. Some ghastly thing with the transmission that a garage will charge a fortune to fix. So we had the car towed to a friend of Jeff's, where Jeff can work on it himself. And then *finally* we came back here to get *my* car and I went in to change clothes because I got grease all over my dress before the tow truck came."

Shelley's somewhat disorganized tale of woe came out in a breathless rush directed at Jan, but she was really looking at Logan, staring at him, Jan realized with sinking dismay, with shocked recognition.

Jan's gaze followed Shelley's. Not once since those first strained moments when she'd given him the check had she given any thought to Logan's status as a paid, professional escort. She had been too overwhelmed by his rugged charm, his consideration, the man-woman electricity that sizzled between them . . . and the sweet-tender fire of his lovemaking.

Now the real truth hit her like a plunge into ice water. He was charming and considerate because it was his *business* to be charming and considerate. It was his *job* to make a woman believe she was supremely desirable. And his expert lovemaking . . .

Jan gave her own small gasp of stunned shock at the ugly possibilities that thought opened up.

Shelley was edging away now, chattering with her usual bubbly brightness about still trying to make it to Jeff's parents' place that night. But she kept looking at Logan as if she couldn't quite believe her eyes.

Finally Shelley was gone, but Jan still stood there staring after the departing car.

"I take it that was your roommate?" Logan asked lightly. "She seemed a little nervous."

Jan realized that she had been so flustered by the unexpected encounter that she had neglected the usual courtesy of introductions. But introductions were hardly necessary, she thought grimly. It was all too obvious that Shelley knew exactly who Jan's escort was.

"It's getting late," Logan prodded gently as Jan continued to stand there, making no move to unlock the door. He reached for the key in her hand, and she jerked back as if she had been electrically shocked.

"I—I've changed my mind." She backed toward the door. "It's been a—a lovely evening. Thank you."

"Jan, what the hell?" Under the harsh glare of the yard light Logan looked more puzzled than angry.

"I just remembered I have things to do tomorrow . . . lots of things to do," she added a little desperately. "And I'm driving into L. A. tomorrow evening for my date with Paul, of course."

"Of course. *Paul.*" Logan's mouth tightened to a harsh line. "And running into your roommate suddenly reminded you of all this?"

Jan abruptly dropped the evasive excuses for her sudden change of heart. "Shelley knows who you are, Logan. She knows . . . *what* you are."

Logan paused a long moment, his expression coldly inscrutable, but Jan could sense the explosive thoughts flashing behind the harsh mask of his face. "I'm afraid I fail to understand why that should have any effect on our spending the night together."

Perhaps it shouldn't, Jan thought wildly, but it *did*. A picture of the shocked look on Shelley's face hung in Jan's mind like a television image caught frozen in a moment in time.

"I take it you think Shelley's opinion of me is something less than favorable?" Logan asked. When Jan still didn't answer, he pursued ruthlessly, "And what Shelley and others think is important to you? More important than your own feelings? More important than what happened between us tonight?"

"No! I don't think so—I don't know!" Jan said helplessly.

"You've changed your mind about wanting to stay all night with me because someone else might disapprove or be shocked or whatever the hell it is you're afraid of." Anger had overtaken his surprise.

No, Jan hadn't changed her mind about *wanting* to spend the night with him. Her body still held the warm imprint of his, still felt lush and soft in the afterglow of his passionate lovemaking. The thought of sleeping snuggled into the lean curve of his body and waking with his arms around her sent a spiral of longing curling deep inside her. And yet . . . "Logan, I—I just need a little time to think."

"About what? What do you plan to do, run my assets and liabilities through a computer the way Paul would, before you decide to spend the night with me?"

"You're being unfair! You're not giving me a chance to explain."

He folded his arms across the formidable wall of his chest. "Explain." His voice was flat. "Explain to me why you changed your mind about staying all night with me. Perhaps you can borrow a few of the phrases Paul used when he explained why he decided not to marry you."

"This isn't like that!"

"Isn't it? Maybe I made a mistake about you," he said harshly. He looked at her in a way that made her feel as if she had shriveled inches in his sight. "Maybe a ruthlessly ambitious bastard like Paul is exactly the type of man you deserve."

He turned on his heel and strode away without glancing

back, and the roar of the powerful engine was audible from blocks away. Jan stood there, frozen, until the sound finally died away in the night.

The usually cozy apartment felt hollow and empty when she went inside. She wavered between anger at Logan and exasperation with herself. Then she added a few more angers. At Shelley. And Jeff. And Jeff's car. Why, why of all nights, *tonight* . . .

And then she had to sigh and face the fact that if the encounter hadn't happened tonight, it would have happened another time. Well, what did it matter, she asked herself defiantly. Just because Logan earned his living rather differently from most men didn't make him reprehensible. For a moment, she felt a surge of defiant, almost fierce protectiveness toward him.

Then she had to give a rueful, humorless laugh at that thought. As if a man like Logan, supremely self-assured, handsome, commanding both in physique and character, as if a man like that ever needed *protection*. No, *she* was the one who needed protection. Protection from him. Protection from the passionate feelings he aroused in her, feelings she was half-afraid already went beyond passion to something deeper and more compelling . . . and frightening . . .

Jan cleaned the apartment the next morning, rushing at a furious pace through vacuuming, scrubbing and dusting. But none of the frantic activity succeeded in keeping her thoughts away from Logan, or away from Shelley's shocked expression when she saw him. Jan held a continuing series of imaginary dialogues with Shelley, sometimes stubbornly defending Logan, sometimes dismissing his occupation negligently, sometimes announcing that she was in love with him and defying Shelley to make something of *that*. She barely thought about her evening date with Paul, and it was with reluctance that she finally realized it was time to start getting ready.

Her enthusiasm for the evening with Paul had not increased by the time she was on the freeway headed toward L. A. It occurred to her that this was all too reminiscent of times gone by, that this was exactly how her former relationship with Paul had operated—at *his* convenience.

As arranged, Paul met her at a small cocktail lounge where they had a drink and then went on to the barbecue together. The party was being given by a Dave and Francine Edwards. Dave was in the finance department of Paul's company. Their home was typical California ranch-style, with a kidney-shaped pool and gas-fired barbecue. Paul introduced Jan around. She had earlier suspected that this evening might be some sort of test to see if she fit in with Paul's friends now, but with surprise she realized that wasn't it at all. Paul was showing her off proudly.

The evening was pleasant enough, the food what Jan always thought of as Californian-Mexican, bearing only a tenuous relationship to the real Mexican food she had eaten on her travels with Adele. The barbecued chicken had a spicy, slightly Spanish-flavored sauce, and the guacamole-topped salads were piled on individual tortillas. The drinks were enormous tequila-based margaritas in salt-rimmed glasses. Jan declined after the first one, remembering her later drive back to Ventura.

She swam in the pool, aware of numerous appreciative male glances at her slim figure in the white suit that made her skin look honey-gold. She was equally aware that Paul noted, and approved of, the complimentary glances. Jan didn't feel at all out of place among his friends and business associates. She could hold her own in conversations with both the men and women. Six years ago, the situation would have awed and intimidated her, but now she felt at ease and somehow not particularly thrilled by it all.

There was an undercurrent to the party that she found vaguely troubling, a certain wariness, as if the people were slightly on guard against each other. At first she took this to be because of a rivalry and competitiveness within the company hierarchy, a certain jockeying for position, but an overheard conversation suddenly made her suspect that the wariness was more personally directed at Paul. She had figured out that he was the highest-ranking company official present.

She overheard the conversation in the poolside cabana,

which had several cubicles separated by gay, striped terrycloth. Jan changed clothes in one cubicle after her swim and went out just as two other women were going inside to dress. A moment later, realizing she had left her lipstick in the cabana, Jan returned. The women obviously did not hear her enter.

"She seems really nice, don't you think?" a voice from one cubicle said. "Is she from here or back east?"

Jan retrieved her lipstick and turned to go, but the next words stopped her.

"Ventura, I think," a second woman replied. "I think someone said she has a TV show up there."

They were talking about her! Jan realized guiltily that she should duck out quietly, but curiosity held her. Paul must have told people she was on TV, which wasn't exactly true—at least, not yet.

"She does seem nice," the second woman went on, but then her voice lowered to a confidential tone. "But I'd certainly be careful what I said around her. You know how Paul Callison got his promotion and transfer out here, don't you?"

The voices went on with some rumors about how Paul had appropriated someone else's marketing idea and presented it as his own. When the idea proved highly successful, he was rewarded with the promotion to the position of assistant supervisor for the West Coast. If true, it was hardly an ethical way to climb the corporate ladder.

Jan tried to dismiss the gossip. After all, it *was* just rumor. But it troubled her anyway.

After dancing on the patio, the party broke up about midnight. When Jan and Paul headed toward their cars, parked together in the circular driveway, Paul suggested that they go somewhere for another drink.

"Thanks, but I don't think so, Paul," Jan said quickly. "I have the drive back to Ventura, and—"

"That's what I want to talk to you about." Paul's words and meaningful tone sent an unmistakable message. He reached for her hands. "There's no need for you to drive all the way back to Ventura tonight."

Jan ignored the obvious suggestion that she spend the night with him. The night air was silky and sweetly scented with the fragrance of early spring blossoms. It was a night for romance, but Jan didn't feel at all romantic. "Paul, I overheard something tonight that's bothering me."

"Oh?" Through his hands clasping hers she felt him stiffen slightly. "About the divorce?"

The divorce? Jan felt a twinge of surprise. What was there about his divorce that might bother her? She hesitated, tempted to ask, then pursued her original point. "No, not about the divorce." They both got into her car, and she went on to repeat what she had heard, feeling guilty even as she did so. Gossip was all too often cruel and malicious, to say nothing of inaccurate, and she should have dismissed it immediately. And yet...

"Rumors and gossip run through any company like wildfire," Paul scoffed, a frown creasing his high forehead. "I got the promotion other people wanted. Every man has to come up with some reason to explain to his wife why someone else got a promotion and he didn't."

"I suppose so," Jan agreed slowly. "But this was so specific. Something about a marketing idea—"

"Who the hell was saying this stuff anyway?" Paul demanded angrily.

It suddenly occurred to Jan that, in Paul's position of authority, he could make it very rough on someone beneath him. And he might very well choose to do so. She was glad that she had no idea who the women or their husbands were and could say so honestly. Paul's scowl disappeared, as if he'd made a deliberate decision to erase it.

"Most people don't realize that any workable idea results from a joint or team effort. The germ of an idea may be good but totally useless until it's"—Paul hesitated for a brief moment—"until it's made viable by someone who knows how to develop it. And then others are jealous or vindictive because they didn't have the foresight or perceptiveness to develop the idea. I'm a doer, Jan, not a dreamer."

He was admitting obliquely that there was a kernel of truth in the women's poolside gossip. This still troubled

Jan, but she also knew that what he said about vindictiveness and jealousy could be true. Paul put an arm around her shoulders.

"Do you understand what I'm trying to say, Jan?" he asked earnestly. "An idea really belongs to the person who knows how to use it. If you're going to get ahead, you have to know how to use an idea, no matter where it originates."

Jan nodded and abruptly dismissed the whole incident from her mind. She really didn't know the facts on either side and was in no position to judge. "I really must be going," she said briskly, putting the key in the ignition.

"Jan . . ." Before she realized what Paul intended, his arm tightened around her shoulders, and he pulled her to him. She resisted for a moment, then, with a kind of detached curiosity, accepted his kiss. He went through all the proper motions, she noted. His mouth moved aggressively against hers, and his tongue probed tentatively. But she felt no more reaction than she would to a handshake from a stranger. When his hand fumbled for her breast, she jerked abruptly away from him.

"Stay with me tonight, Jan." He was breathing rapidly, and his voice had a hoarse note. "I need you."

Stay with me tonight. It was the second time in little more than twenty-four hours that Jan had heard those words. This time she wasn't even remotely tempted to say yes. She felt, in fact, a distinct repugnance at the idea of staying with Paul. She pushed him away gently as he tried to embrace her again.

"I don't think so, Paul."

He drew back and made a pretense of straightening his tie. "Very well," he said stiffly. "I realize you may feel some bitterness about what happened in the past. If it will make you feel better to let me suffer awhile now—"

"No. It isn't that."

"I'm interested in marrying you now, Jan." He sounded reproving, almost as if he were chiding her for having indiscreet thoughts. "I think we could make a fantastic team together."

Marriage to Paul. The dream she had once lived for. Now it was within her reach.

"Paul, it's all over," she said, gently but firmly. She didn't even feel any desire to retaliate and hurt him as he had once hurt her. She simply felt neutral toward him now. He had no power to arouse emotion of any kind within her anymore.

He glowered at her in a kind of helpless frustration, as if he knew she was beyond his reach. "It's that guy you were with at the wedding, isn't it?"

Jan turned the ignition key and started the engine. "Good-bye, Paul."

With a muttered oath he slid out of the car, flinging something back at her that she assumed was insultingly derogatory. She neither knew nor cared what it was.

She soared along the highway toward Ventura with an incredible sense of freedom. The final cord to that unhappy period in her past—a slim cord she hadn't realized still existed—had been severed, and she was totally, exhilaratingly free. She felt as if she were soaring as high as the moon sailing grandly overhead, the same moon that had looked down on the magic of her lovemaking with Logan . . .

As Paul had accused her, did Logan have something to do with her rejection of Paul? Coming back to earth from her soaring celebration of freedom, she considered the thought carefully and concluded that, except for the coincidence of timing, there was no connection. She would have rejected Paul even if she had never met Logan. The love she had once felt was long-vanished, though she was no longer so certain now that what she had felt six years ago had really been love.

She had the feeling that she was hovering precariously on the brink of something of far greater depth and magnitude with Logan. But if that were true, why did she dread the thought of facing Shelley's shocked and curious questions? Why couldn't she simply shrug and dismiss her roommate's opinions as immaterial?

Suddenly external opinions became immaterial as the

realization struck Jan with a shattering blow that her arguments with herself were of no consequence. She had been wrapped up in her own feelings, in the turmoil of her own doubts. But all her agonizing soul searching was irrelevant. She had no choices to make regarding Logan. He had made the choice. With a scathing indictment of her values, he had walked out on her!

CHAPTER
Six

JAN WAS IN bed before Shelley returned to the apartment late Sunday evening, and she didn't get up until after Shelley left for work Monday morning. She had absolutely no regrets about having broken off with Paul, but some of her giddy exhilaration was dampened by a dispirited inner fog. She was neither ashamed nor regretful about that magical interlude of love on Logan's sailboat, but she still dreaded facing Shelley. And hated herself for feeling that way.

She passed through various stages in her thoughts, from hoping that she had been wrong in thinking Shelley had recognized Logan, to hoping Shelley's own weekend had been so marvelous—or atrocious—that she had entirely forgotten the encounter outside the apartment Friday night.

When Shelley walked into the apartment after work Monday, Jan knew neither was the case.

"Jan, how come you never *told* me you were dating Logan Pierce?" Shelley demanded without preliminaries.

Jan tried to be nonchalant. "It really didn't seem important. Would you like a cup of tea? I'm fixing meatloaf for supper, and it won't be done for a while yet."

A fragrant aroma wafted out from the kitchen, but Shelley paid no attention. "January McFarland, don't you try to sidetrack me with tea and meatloaf," Shelley said threateningly. "Where did you meet him? And why didn't you tell me?"

"I went to that art exhibit in L. A. a couple of weeks ago, remember? He was there with Mrs. Farrington, and I recognized him from your description. I would never have talked to him under ordinary circumstances, of course, but I just *had* to have a man to take along to the wedding in Bakersfield. At least I thought I had to . . . though, as it turned out, it really wasn't important at all. But that's another matter." Jan paused for breath in the frantic race of words before rushing on. "So anyway I hired him to go to the wedding with me, and then there was this mix-up about my paying him, and when I called him about it, he invited me to dinner and I . . . went."

Jan's voice ran down to an awkward ending while Shelley just stared at her.

"Jan, what in the *hell* are you talking about?" Shelley finally asked, both her words and her slow, bewildered tone totally uncharacteristic of her. "Are you trying to tell me that you *paid* Logan Pierce to go to the wedding in Bakersfield with you?"

Jan tried to give a negligent, sophisticated laugh, but it came out a nervous rattle. "I decided that, if hiring a paid escort was good enough for Mrs. Farrington, it was good enough for me too. And it really worked out very well," she added defensively.

Shelley's expression had gone from perplexed to *peculiar*. She hadn't even kicked off her shoes the way she always did when she first got home. "What on earth made you think Logan Pierce was a paid escort?"

"You had described this 'gorgeous hunk' you saw with

Mrs. Farrington in Santa Barbara. The intense blue eyes. The muscles. The burnt-gold hair. The 'animal magnetism.' So, of course, when I saw Mrs. Farrington with Logan at the art exhibit, I knew he had to be her paid escort. He fit your description exactly."

"Yes, I suppose he does have the physique. And the hair. And the eyes. And everything else I described. But..." Shelley kept shaking her head negatively all the time her words confirmed the description. "A 'gorgeous hunk' is a—a mindless mass of muscle held together by a tan and his own ego! The male version of the beautiful-but-dumb blonde. And that does *not* describe Logan Pierce!"

"Shelley, just what are you trying to tell me?"

"Jan, how could you possibly have thought that *Logan Pierce* was a—" The horrified look in Shelley's eyes suddenly changed to bubbling merriment, and she gave a whoop of laughter. "Oh, Jan, that is priceless, absolutely priceless! To think you *hired* Logan Pierce—and he actually went and took the *money.*"

"Yes, of course." Jan was beginning to get annoyed with Shelley's strange reaction. "I gave him a check."

"Jan, do you know what you've *done?*"

"Something that you obviously find very amusing," Jan said sourly. She had been prepared for a curious, shocked reaction from Shelley—perhaps a certain wide-eyed distaste, but certainly not this almost bawdy amusement.

"Jan, you hired a man who is one of the most sought-after bachelors in the whole country, a man half the women in Ventura would walk from here to L. A. to date. He has a gorgeous home out in the Ojai Valley, and he's president of the family-owned corporation, with offices over in Oxnard, and they own all kinds of companies and businesses. Jan, he isn't one of Mrs. F.'s paid escorts, he's her nephew!"

Jan dropped numbly to the edge of the sofa. "No, no, you must be mistaken," she protested. "Are you *sure?*" she asked, her voice rising on a note of panic when the vehement shake of Shelley's head denied any possibility of mistake.

"Of course I'm sure. He comes in the office once in a while to see Mrs. F., and he leaves a trail of swooning secretaries and typists behind him."

Jan knew Shelley was exaggerating, of course, but she didn't doubt that Logan's dazzling good looks and formidable physique raised havoc with the female office staff at Buenaventura Development.

"But you looked so shocked when you saw him," Jan protested, as if by arguing she could still convince Shelley she was wrong. "I thought you were shocked because you recognized him as Mrs. Farrington's paid escort."

"I was shocked at seeing *my* roommate with Logan Pierce. There's an account executive at the office who would *kill* to go out with him." Shelley paused, her head cocked speculatively. "Did he stay all night?"

"Of course not!"

Jan rushed out to the kitchen and flung open the oven door to hide the incriminating stain spreading over her face. No, Logan hadn't stayed all night. She'd fallen into bed with him before the night had barely started!

Jan rushed from stove to table to refrigerator, slicing the meatloaf, tossing a salad, slapping sour cream and chives on the baked potatoes—all in a frantic rush to avoid the horrible sense of embarrassment swooping down on her.

But when they were finally sitting at the tiny dinette, Jan couldn't eat a thing. "How could I have made such an incredible mistake?" she groaned. Her thoughts went back to that initial meeting at the art exhibit. Logan must have thought she was out of her mind! And then to call him at his home . . . She writhed inwardly, impaled by humiliation. It was like a ghastly dream of walking naked among a crowd of fully-dressed strangers. Only this was no dream. She had done it. "I'll never live it down. I feel as if I want to crawl in a hole and disappear forever."

"Well, you certainly couldn't have done it without some cooperation from *him*," Shelley observed. She piled ketchup on the meatloaf and downed a hearty forkful. "I wonder why he didn't tell you right off you'd made a silly mistake."

Jan suddenly fixed Shelley with a threatening glare. "Shelley, if you ever tell anyone about this, and I mean *anyone* . . ."

"Of course I won't," Shelley said blithely.

Jan reached over and grabbed Shelley's wrist. "No, I mean it, Shelley. I know how things spill out of you. You have to promise me you'll keep this secret."

Shelley looked injured, but then seemed to realize how upset Jan really was. She reached over and squeezed Jan's other hand. "Hon, I promise. Honestly I do. I know I tend to blabber on, but if it really, *really* matters, no one will ever hear a word about it from me."

Jan returned the squeeze and relaxed slightly. She recognized the strength of Shelley's promise. In spite of Shelley's usually impulsive chatter, the secret was safe with her.

"But if it were me, I don't think I'd want to keep it a secret," Shelley said, her blue eyes dancing again. "Really, the joke is on him. You pulled off this absolutely marvelous *coup*. How many women have tried sneaky subterfuges to get a date with him, and failed? But you succeeded, and you're going to have a canceled check to prove it. If it were me, I'd have the check framed!"

Jan smiled weakly. She supposed it was rather humorous, in a way. Mistaking a man of Logan Pierce's status and caliber for a—a gigolo! The thought suddenly struck Jan that all the things Logan had told Paul about who and what he was, things Jan thought were merely audacious lies, were all *true*. There was nothing phony at all about his commanding air of self-assurance or his dynamic presence. Oh, how, *how* could she ever have made such a colossal Grand Canyon–scale error? The car, the clothes, the home near Ojai, the immediate recognition of Paul's company...all bespoke a man of authority and money. She cringed with the humiliation of it. It was the social gaffe to end all social gaffes.

Looking back, Jan had no doubt now that her initial approach at the art exhibit had surprised Logan. He must have realized on the phone that she had made a ridiculous mistake. Why hadn't he told her then who he really was? Why had he gone along with the preposterous farce of being a paid escort? Why had he let her make a complete fool of herself?

The first answer that jabbed into Jan's mind was that, once over his initial shock, Logan must have thought her outrageous error quite amusing. A titillating story with which to entertain his sophisticated friends, with a spicy postscript about the sailboat interlude?

Jan considered the thought suspiciously, but then dismissed it. Logan Pierce might be the subject of considerable speculative gossip, but he wasn't the type to spread or start gossip himself. He had too much self-confidence to feel the need to brag about his exploits or conquests.

But the fact remained, she thought unhappily, that she *was* a conquest. Shelley saw the situation as a delicious little game, the stuff of which light comedies were made, but Shelley didn't know the full extent of the stakes in this game. Jan had made love with Logan because she felt something for him, both physically and emotionally. She had shared a deep and meaningful part of herself with him. But Logan had made love with her—why? Because he was a male and she a reasonably attractive, ready, and willing female. And then he'd had the nerve to get angry when she became not quite so willing and changed her mind about spending the night with him!

Jan alternated between anger and hurt and a feeling that the best thing would be to simply put the whole unlikely situation out of her mind. "Chalk this one up to experience," as Logan had so scathingly announced he intended to do.

She might have been able to do that were it not for two things. One was the gut-wrenching feeling that Logan had taken something from her that went beyond sexual exploitation. She had confided in him, told him things she had never told anyone else, revealed intimate facts not only about her relationship with Paul but also about herself and her own deepest self-doubts and insecurities and vulnerabilities. And it wasn't as if she had particularly *wanted* to share her painful secrets with anyone. Logan had deftly pried the confidences out of her, and he had done it under false pretenses, pretending to be so sympathetic and understanding, pretending to be someone he wasn't. It left Jan feeling vulnerably exposed, as if the glossy shell she had carefully constructed around herself had been expertly and clinically sandpapered away to reveal the raw sensitivity underneath. He *knew* her, she thought unhappily, knew her in every basic sense of the word.

The other reason she couldn't just "chalk it up to experience" was that, just about the time she worked herself into a self-righteous fury with Logan, some other unwanted memory would slip into her mind. Logan bringing her rolls and juice at the Bakersfield motel, Logan smiling at her over a jeweled glass of wine, Logan sweeping her to dizzying heights with kisses and caresses.

The following midafternoon, as much in an attempt to get her mind off Logan as anything, Jan drove out to Ojai again. The day was glorious, southern California at its tourist-brochure best. The mountains beyond Ojai were snow-dusted, the air sun-washed and fresh. The small town itself was a combination of old-fashioned elegance and dusty charm, but with an undertone of bustle. In the middle of town was pleasant Libbey Park, shaded with magnificent old spreading oaks. A fountain bubbled in the open courtyard. Beside the park was the historic old post-office tower that housed Ojai's bell chimes. Across from the park was a shaded arcade of stores and boutiques.

However, most of the inviting scene was wasted on Jan. She stalked up to the blocky two-story television-station building on the edge of town. Being in Ojai served only to remind her that Logan Pierce lived somewhere nearby, and she resented that he had all this to enjoy.

Jan was also dismayed to find that the friendly receptionist who had previously been at the front desk was not there. In her place was the lush brunette whom Jan had noted on a couple of news features. Her aloof expression was anything but welcoming.

Jan put on her warmest smile. "Hello! You're Stephanie Trainer, aren't you? Your news feature on the sailboat races the other night was really interesting."

"Thank you. I'm just filling in at the front desk while the regular receptionist has the flu." The girl's icy expression thawed slightly, and she made a small grimace of distaste, as if she felt the temporary position were beneath her. "May I help you?"

"I'm January McFarland."

Stephanie's expression changed by little more than a flicker of her long eyelashes, but Jan had the distinct impression the girl recognized the name—and didn't welcome it. Jan hesitated a moment, then altered her plan of approach warily.

"Has a new station manager been hired yet?" she asked.

"No."

"Mr. Gurley is still in charge?"

"The station management is temporarily under direct control of the parent company."

"I see." And what, Jan wondered suspiciously, did that stilted mumbo-jumbo mean? "May I speak with the person in charge then?"

"About?"

"A position on the staff."

"The clerical department does its own hiring. Second floor."

Jan leaned her palms on the desk separating her from the dark-haired girl. "I'm not looking for a typing job, Miss Trainer, as I'm sure you are very well aware!"

"There are no openings at present." Stephanie Trainer remained unruffled by Jan's outburst. Her dark eyes held a glitter that looked suspiciously like triumph, as if she were pleased that she had managed to discompose Jan.

Why, Jan wondered, her annoyance tinged with puzzlement. She certainly had never done anything to Stephanie Trainer. Or was Stephanie simply one of those women who automatically considered every other attractive woman an enemy? Jan took a controlling breath. "I'd prefer to discuss the possibility of an opening with the manager."

"If you want to see the manager, you'll have to fill out a standard job-application form first." Stephanie's voice was complacent now, as if she were repeating some law as unbreakable as gravity.

"My records are already on file! I was supposed to be working here by now."

Stephanie Trainer turned to a gray filing cabinet and riffled manila folders with her long fingernails. "I don't find anything."

Jan nibbled her lower lip in frustration. Actually, there probably wasn't any job-application file on her. The important information on her had probably been stored in Warren Anderson's head. And had died with him. She had the unhappy feeling she might never get beyond this front desk again.

She gritted her teeth. "Very well. I'll fill out an application."

Stephanie Trainer handed her an application form, which Jan, in her anger and frustration, promptly ruined. She seethed under the humiliation of having to ask Stephanie for another form. Stephanie flicked the paper across the desk with just enough force to send it skittering to the floor. Jan was forced to stoop and pick up the paper. Stephanie flashed her a brilliantly lethal smile.

Jan struggled to keep calm and fill out the form correctly. When she came to the block marked education, she hesitated. One glance at Stephanie told Jan that the other girl was surely the product of some prestigious university. Jan tapped the table indecisively with her ball-point pen, then defiantly gave herself a degree in communications from a Midwestern university located near where her parents now lived. As Paul had said, no one would ever check. She hurried on quickly to the more secure footing of outlining her television experience with Adele Meeker in Phoenix. At the bottom of the sheet, she added a few comments about her previous contacts with Warren Anderson.

Stephanie accepted the application as if it were a soiled handkerchief.

"You will see that the manager sees the application as soon as possible?" Jan asked suspiciously.

"Yes, of course. You needn't bother to call us. We'll call—"

Jan stalked out before Stephanie could finish the cliché. Walking to the car, Jan found her hands clenched in hard knots. Her temper, still simmering under the outrage of what

Logan Pierce had done, had mounted dangerously during the puzzling encounter with Stephanie Trainer. And her temper did not improve when she reached her car and found one side sagging with a flat tire.

"Damn, damn, damn," she muttered under her breath. Well, she had changed a flat tire before. She opened the hatchback and dug out the necessary tools. Where was a gentleman when you needed one, she thought sourly, eyeing the parking lot which was empty of human life. She got the car jacked up and pried off the hubcap. She was perspiring by the time she finally got the first lug nut off. But the next one absolutely would not budge. The tire had last been changed in a garage, and the lug nuts tightened by machine. There was nothing to do but walk to a service station and wait around until an attendant was free to return with her.

It was well past dark by the time Jan's car was roadworthy again. She washed her hands with cold water and gritty soap in the service station's restroom and decided that she needed a cup of coffee to calm her nerves before driving back to Ventura.

The restaurant was small and clean, the waitress pleasant, but the first thing Jan did was slosh a darkening stain of coffee on the sleeve of her linen jacket, right next to a slash of grease from the tire. Suddenly everything that had gone wrong on this miserable day coalesced into an explosion of fury with Logan Pierce. She was *not* going to let him get away with what he'd done. She was going to tell him exactly what she thought of a man who accepted a woman's innermost confidences under false pretenses, tricked and exploited and took advantage of her in the most despicable way possible.

Jan motioned the waitress over and asked if she knew where Logan Pierce lived. After a brief consultation with someone on the other side of a swinging door, the woman returned with directions.

On the drive out through the valley, Jan planned exactly what she intended to say to Logan Pierce, a brilliant, fiery dialogue of accusation and condemnation that would make him think twice before he took advantage of some other unsuspecting girl. By the time she reached the address, even the impressive stone arch over the paved driveway failed to intimidate her. The driveway led between low stone walls overhung by lush, glossy-leaved avocado trees. The split-level house was Spanish-style, with a tiled roof and the graceful curve of an arched entryway. A planting of flaming-red torch ginger accented the entryway. Light fanned upward from somewhere behind the house, giving it a soft, mellow halo.

Jan felt her first moment of doubt as she eyed the double-entry doors of dark, carved wood flanked by wrought-iron lanterns. Maybe she shouldn't...

Yes, she should, she thought defiantly as she slammed the car door with more force than necessary. Logan Pierce wasn't going to get away unscathed with what he had done.

She punched the doorbell decisively. A middle-aged Hispanic woman opened the door. Jan held a momentary mental debate with herself about giving a phony name, thinking Logan might would simply refuse to see her if she revealed her true identity.

"Would you please tell Mr. Pierce that Janet Monroe would like to see him," she finally said, holding her head high.

The woman disappeared, leaving Jan in the cool elegance of the Mexican tilted foyer. A Spanish-style wrought-iron chandelier cast a golden glow of light around her. A painting of a sleepy mission church decorated one wall. The time seemed interminable before the woman returned and requested that Jan come with her.

They went down a long, wide hallway that finally opened onto a swimming pool underlit with a soft rainbow of light. A wing of the house extended the length of the pool and angled around the far side, ending in a half-circle of dimly lit glass. The woman led Jan to the glassed-in area, opened the door, nodded politely, and departed.

The glass walls dripped with a lush cascade of hanging plants, and Logan Pierce stood immersed to mid-chest in a sunken octagonal hot tub in the center of the small jungle. His arms were stretched out along the rim of tub. The water, driven by unseen jets, swirled and bubbled around him as a steamy mist rose from the surface.

Jan's defiant self-confidence floundered, and the only thought that was crystal-clear in her mind at the moment was that Logan was surely naked in the tub. She felt a sudden beading of perspiration that came from something other than the steamy warmth of the room. Logan gave her a lazy smile. He didn't seem surprised that Janet Monroe was really January McFarland.

"Care to join me?" he invited amiably.

"No!"

She was looking down on him. She was fully clothed and angrily psyched up for this counter. He was naked and unprepared. Under the circumstances, she should have held a supreme advantage, yet she didn't. She already felt on the defensive, and all her cutting barbs and devastating condemnations tangled in her mind like so much limp spaghetti.

"And to what do I owe the pleasure of this unexpected visit?" Logan asked with mocking politeness. His hard-muscled body was an indistinct bronze shimmer undulating gently in the roiling water. The damp, dark gold hair on his exposed chest had a crisp, independent curl. She tried not to remember how it had felt brushing against her naked breasts.

"I—I wanted to talk to you." She had a strangely dizzy sensation as she looked down at him, as if she might slowly tilt and plunge helplessly into the water with him. She made a concerted grab for control of both herself and the situation. "I'm sure you never expected me to show up here at your home."

"I invited you to spend the night here, remember? Or have you forgotten already?" His soft voice hardened as he added, "No doubt you had a busy and—ummm—distracting weekend in L. A. with Paul."

Jan opened her mouth to snap a cutting retort that she most certainly had not spent the weekend with Paul, then pressed her lips together abruptly. She wasn't about to admit to Logan that he had been one hundred percent right about Paul. The fact that he was right—infuriatingly right—suddenly recharged the faltering batteries of her anger.

"And what would you have done if I had come? Passed me around among your friends as the girl so desperate for a man that she was willing to *pay* for one? That must have given you a marvelous laugh." Jan's own laugh was bitter. "You took advantage of me."

Logan straightened slowly in the hot tub. "I never took advantage of a woman in my life," he said evenly. "Physically or otherwise."

"You did! You pretended to be something you weren't. I confided in you. I told you everything! You encouraged me . . . And to you it was all just some amusing game. Why didn't you tell me who you were, Logan? Why did you let me go on and on making a fool of myself? Why did you—"

He was getting out of the hot tub, rising out of the bubbling water like a mystical bronzed water animal. His powerful chest was half-turned from her to reveal a ripple of back muscles and his golden chest hair narrowed to a single line on his hard-muscled abdomen. Then, with a feeling that was half-disappointment, half-relief, Jan saw the flash of a brief band of white swim trunks. He wasn't naked after all. With a strange fascination, she watched the wet tracks his feet left as he moved with silent swiftness toward her. A golden panther in a green jungle setting leaving strangely human tracks . . .

"Did you think I was naked?" he asked mockingly as he stood before her, tall and tanned and almost savagely male. She didn't answer, but they both knew the slow stain that crept over her face was answer enough. "Maria would never have allowed you through the door unless I met her minimum standards of—ah—decency for a proper young lady's eyes."

Jan ignored the lightly mocking words. "You lied to me," she accused. Her voice was barely above a whisper.

His hands caught her just above the elbows. Moisture and warmth seeped through the sleeves of her linen jacket. "I never told you anything but the truth. You chose not to believe me."

Her mind skimmed unevenly over snatches of conversation, broken images of scenes. Perhaps he hadn't actually lied...."It was all just part of the game you were playing! Was that one of the amusing little rules you set up for yourself? No lying? But sometimes not telling all the truth is worse than outright lying!"

He shook her lightly, his jaws clenched as if he had to exert iron control not to take out the full violence of his rising anger on her. The movement showered her with a spray of droplets from his wet hair and body. "I suppose I should have told you," he admitted grudgingly. "I started to tell you Friday night, and then I figured it could wait until the next morning. How did you find out who I am?"

"My roommate recognized you. At the time I thought she recognized you as the paid escort she'd seen with Mrs. Farr—" Jan broke off in the middle of the incriminating name.

She waited, her breath held, for the shocking truth about his aunt to hit him. His naked chest was only inches away, and she had to fight a strange desire to lean forward and let the tips of her breasts rest against the solid, tanned expanse. Her own fully-clothed state seemed to magnify the raw virility of his near nakedness. In spite of the steamy heat of the room, she felt a shivery thrill of danger. She tensed, not knowing whether to expect a kiss or a teeth-rattling shake from him.

Unexpectedly, Logan did neither. Instead he threw back his head and laughed, a roar of genuine amusement. "Leave it to Aunt Rue," he murmured. "I figured it had to be something like that."

"You know about your aunt's..."

"Hired escorts? Oh, yes. She isn't all that discreet about them. You needn't look so horrified," Logan added, smiling down into Jan's startled eyes. "Aunt Rue has this—ummm—unique sense of humor. She enjoys giving people a jolt now and then with something like revealing that her date is really a paid escort."

"How...unusual," Jan echoed. She swallowed. "But still, you should have told me. You shouldn't have let me go on and on with my ridiculous mistake." Her throat tightened as more intimate memories flooded her mind. "And you shouldn't have——"

"Jan, listen to me." His hands slid down to her waist. Neither of them paid any attention to the dark lines of dampness his wet thighs left on her skirt as he pulled her closer. "I noticed you when I first saw you at the art exhibit. You looked so cool and beautiful and poised. And then you went tumbling toward the painting, and I saw something of the little girl underneath, fresh and sweet and maybe just a little bit klutzy."

Jan grimaced. "Gee, thanks," she muttered.

He lifted one hand to smooth the damp tendrils of hair that curled against her temple in the humid atmosphere. "I liked what I saw. Then when you came over and asked for my phone number, I didn't know quite what to think. I suppose I'm basically an old-fashioned type who figures that the male makes the first move."

She remembered his welcoming look, then the not-quite-complimentary reappraisal when she asked for his phone number. "Then why did you give me your number?"

His smoothly muscled shoulders moved in a slight shrug. "Maybe because I wondered whether you'd really have the nerve to call. Maybe because I was still interested in spite of being put off by your . . . forwardness."

Forwardness! Jan had never in her life used even the old I-just-happened-to-have-two-tickets-to-a-play routine to ask a man for a date, let alone had the nerve to issue a point-blank invitation.

"Then, when you called, I finally figured out what had happened—that somehow you had mistaken me for one of Aunt Rue's paid escorts."

"And you thought it was funny," she accused. "You decided to play it for laughs."

"I suppose so," he admitted. "But, at the same time, I couldn't help wondering why such a beautiful woman was desperate enough to hire a date. Do you remember you asked me how I had gotten into my particular 'line of work'?" Jan nodded warily. "And I told you the chance to get into the line of work presented itself and I couldn't resist taking it?" His voice held a husky chuckle.

Jan didn't know quite how they had gotten there, but her arms were resting on his wet shoulders. Her fingertips played lightly with a damp curl at the back of his neck. She still felt angry, still felt betrayed, yet his half-tender, half-amused explanation was having an effect on her. Or was it, she thought a little unsteadily, as he dropped a damp, softly delicious kiss on the corner of her mouth, the effect of his nearness more than his explanation? The feel of his arms around her and his ruggedly male body pressing against her were not conducive to rational thinking. She made a valiant effort to swing her drifting thoughts back on course.

"You took advantage of me," she said doggedly, returning to her earlier accusation. "You exploited me."

"Exploited you?" His voice was still soft, but there was a hint of steel buried somewhere underneath. A bronze-gold eyebrow lifted. "I had the impression the pleasure and satisfaction weren't exactly one-sided. It might be just as fair to say you exploited me."

"That's ridiculous!"

The soft brrr of a wall telephone startled them both. Logan let it ring, but when the noise persisted he reluctantly released her and went to answer it. Jan was grateful for the few moments to try to collect her thoughts. The pieces she had so neatly fit together were coming apart like a carelessly scattered jigsaw puzzle. Even though she was out of Logan's arms, she wasn't out of the sphere of influence of that potent masculinity. His body was leaning at a negligent angle against the cream-colored wall as he talked on the phone, one arm extended as a brace, his bare feet crossed. He was a brazenly magnificent male animal in his near-nudity, lithely poised for action even in the careless stance. Droplets of water glittered like hidden jewels among the fine hairs curling against his sun-darkened chest. When he turned his back to her, her eyes followed the arrowed taper of broad shoulders to lean hips and tautly sculptured buttocks beneath the narrow white band of his swim trunks. She felt a small beading of perspiration on her upper lip. The steamy heat, she thought distractedly. The jungle of plants. The hiss and gurgle of water swirling in the hot tub.

He came back to her, pausing to flick a switch that calmed the bubbling water. "Excuse the interruption. It was Aunt Rue." He smiled lightly. "Perhaps her ears were tingling." He put his arms around Jan again, locking them at the back of her waist as if they belonged there. "Where were we?"

"We were discussing people exploiting other people."

"And what did we decide?" he challenged lightly.

"I—I'm not sure." Jan had the helpless feeling she wasn't quite sure of anything.

"Jan, I admit it wasn't exactly—" He hesitated, searching for the right word. "Wasn't exactly gallant of me to go along with your little mistake, and I did see a certain humor in the situation. But once you told me about Paul and your old relationship with him, I realized it wasn't just fun and games. I . . . cared. I didn't want to see Paul hurt you again. And I damn sure thought you needed a little protection."

Her arms were around his neck again. They seemed to sneak there without any guidance or control from her conscious mind. She felt herself softening, both emotionally and physically. She was standing between his braced legs, conscious of his ready masculinity.

"And Friday night on your sailboat?" she asked tremulously. Her fingertips circled his earlobe. "What were you thinking then?"

"I—"

Whatever he started to say was interrupted by the opening of the inner door to the hot-tub room. A stocky, swarthy-skinned man in blue boxer-style swim trunks started toward the hot tub, then stopped short when he saw Logan and Jan standing together in what Jan suddenly realized was an almost incriminatingly intimate position, in spite of the fact that she was fully clothed.

She glanced up at Logan. There was an odd, uneasy expression on his face. Her glance darted back to the other man, and suddenly she recognized him. Anton Bertanoli, the artist at whose showing in Los Angeles she had first met

Logan. The man was holding his right arm close to his side. He turned back toward the door.

"I will come back later," he said in a softly accented voice.

Logan was still standing there with that same odd expression on his face. With a small sense of shock, Jan realized that he wasn't going to make introductions, even though the rather awkward situation obviously called for the courtesy of introductions. Why not? she wondered with a sharpening sense of suspicion. She slipped recklessly out of the half-circle of Logan's arm before he realized what she was going to do.

"Mr. Bertanoli! How nice to meet you," she exclaimed, just as if Logan had made the proper introductions. "I was so impressed with your exhibit in Los Angeles. You do seascapes and coastal scenes as no one else can."

The dark eyes, almost hooded, widened to a pleased glow. "You're very kind. Thank you. And you are?" He inclined his head politely.

"Just a friend of Logan's. January McFarland." She held out her hand. He shook it awkwardly with his left hand.

"January," he repeated, then added tentatively, "Jan?" When she nodded, he smiled broadly. "I am pleased to meet you. Logan has told me of you."

It took only an instant for the meaning of the words to register on Jan, and then a shock wave hit her. Her eyes met Bertanoli's curious gaze with a kind of horror. Her earlier brief suspicion that Logan might use the story of her ridiculous mistake to entertain his sophisticated friends had been too quickly dismissed. He *had* talked about her with Bertanoli, told him all about the amusing Bakersfield escapade! And the sailboat incident too, no doubt. She had been right. To Logan it was all just some sophisticated game with which to amuse his friends! No wonder he hadn't wanted to make introductions. Logan knew that Bertanoli would recognize her name and make the incriminating connection!

Bertanoli was inspecting her openly now, from her hair curling damply around her face to her rumpled blouse, half out of her skirt. And below the blouse... Jan's eyes followed Bertanoli's. The pale blue linen plainly showed two long, tapered shadows of dampness where Logan's muscular thighs had pressed against her. And centered between and just above them was another pressure mark, so precisely and blatantly placed that she felt her face flame. With a small, strangled gasp of embarrassment and humiliation, Jan fled toward the outer door.

"Jan, come back here!" Logan called imperiously. "I want to talk to you."

"I think you've already talked enough," Jan shot over her shoulder with scorching scorn. "I never want to—to talk to you or see you again!"

He folded his arms across his solid chest. "We'll see about that," he muttered ominously.

CHAPTER
Seven

SOMEHOW JAN MANAGED to stumble around the side of the house and find her car parked in the driveway. She drove back to Ventura with both hands gripping the steering wheel tightly to control their unsteadiness. So much for trying to give Logan a piece of her mind and put him in his place, she thought with bitter ruefulness. The embarrassment and humiliation she had felt earlier were inconsequential compared to that gnawing at her now. He *had* told! He really had talked and laughed about her. *Snickered* was probably a better word, she thought grimly. Bertanoli's broad smile and curious appraisal once he knew her identity had said it all.

The next day, for the first time, Jan gave serious thought to simply packing up and leaving Ventura. She could go back to Phoenix and get some kind of minor job at the television station there and wait for something better to come along. She didn't want to be in the same city... county... state!... with Logan Pierce. Paradoxically, at the very moment she was thinking that, she felt a strange pang of regret and loss in the knowledge that she would never see him again. Not loss for the real Logan Pierce, she assured herself bitterly. Loss for some dream-fantasy man who didn't really exist.

By the following day, Jan was definitely leaning toward retreat to Phoenix. There was nothing for her here, either professionally or personally. She had reached the point of staring undecidedly at her suitcases in the back of the closet when the telephone rang.

In astonishment Jan listened to an unfamiliar but not hostile female voice say that her job application had been reviewed and that the television station manager would like to interview her personally. Would two o'clock this afternoon be convenient?

Jan hesitated momentarily. This was what she had been waiting and hoping for, yet some small part of her warned that she might be better off getting out and putting the whole incredible, humiliating Ventura experience behind her.

No, she decided resolutely. It was Logan from whom she was really considering fleeing, and she wasn't going to let him drive her away or damage her any more deeply than he already had. The job was still a worthwhile opportunity.

Jan was prepared to out-intimidate Stephanie Trainer at the front desk, but the sultry brunette had been replaced by the more friendly regular receptionist named Linda. Linda announced Jan's presence over the phone, then led her through a minor maze of hallways to a closed door.

The man was standing at a window, his back to the door, when Jan stepped inside. He bore a startling resemblance to Logan, Jan thought with a small jolt. Same formidable shoulders that carried a well-cut dark suit with lithe elegance, same lean hips, same burnt-gold hair. There was even a familiar hint of curl where the crisp hair met the back of his neck. Jan gave herself an abrupt mental shake. Her imagination was running away with her, seeing Logan

Pierce in any attractive man. The man turned.

It *was* Logan Pierce!

He smiled pleasantly. "Well, it appears that you changed your mind. You *do* want to see and talk to me again after all."

Jan clenched her jaw to keep it from dropping open. This couldn't be happening. Her erratic thoughts made no more sense than static electricity. "What are you doing here?" she finally managed to gasp.

"We've hired a new manager from back east, but he won't be able to take over for two or three weeks. So I'm temporarily in control as station manager."

"But you . . . the station . . . I don't understand!" She felt strangely disoriented, as if she were on a tilting deck and everything was sliding out of control.

"I believe I mentioned that Pierce-Logan Enterprises has some television and radio interests?" He walked to the desk and negligently riffled through a stack of papers. When she made no sound beyond a choked gasp, he tilted an eyebrow at her questioningly.

Yes, he had mentioned the company's radio and TV interests. But the comment had passed right on by Jan, dismissed as another of his audacious lies. But now everything dropped neatly into place—his true identity as Mrs. Farrington's nephew, Shelley's saying that Mrs. Farrington was a shareholder in the company that owned the station, Logan's claiming a directorship on Mrs. Farrington's Buenaventura Development Company, Stephanie's loftily announcing that the station was temporarily under management of the parent company. It all tied together. Yes, Logan Pierce was in control. No doubt about it.

Then why had he dragged her in here? To personally relish the moment of telling her the station didn't want her? To show her that he could use his money and power to manipulate her at his will?

No way, she thought vehemently. She turned on her heel and headed for the door. With surprising speed, his fingers closed around the doorknob first. At his touch, Jan jerked her hand back as if it had been scalded.

"What do you think you're doing?" Logan demanded.

"I'm not playing any more of your little games. Please open the door."

"You consider a job here at the station a 'game'?"

"You didn't trick me into coming here to discuss a job! You just want your revenge. No one, I assume, walks out on the great Logan Pierce without paying for it!"

"Speaking of paying..." He released the doorknob, though his solid body still guarded the doorway and his eyes targeted her warily. "You didn't give me a chance to return this."

He dug in his wallet and produced her check, folded and a little worn and frayed now. She snatched at the scrap of paper, but he raised his arm, deliberately holding it out of her reach.

"I do rather hate to return it. I thought it might look nice framed on my bedroom wall. A souvenir of the only girl who ever paid me to take her out." Both his voice and his expression as he looked at the check held an exaggerated regret. He gave a theatrical sigh. "A man in my position sometimes suspects that women are only after his money, and it was a real pleasure knowing that this girl was different, that she—"

"Damn it, Logan, just give me the check," Jan muttered through gritted teeth. He lowered the check a few inches and finally, standing on tiptoe, she managed to snatch it. With a few swift rips, she tore the check to shreds and dropped the pieces into a wastebasket.

He looked injured. "If I'd known you were going to do that, I'd have kept the check."

"Is that all?" she asked evenly.

He dropped the lightly mocking air. "Not quite. We still have a position here at the station to discuss." He returned to the desk, the hint of a scowl on his face. He added reluctantly, "And I have a favor to ask of you."

"I was under the impression Logan Pierce *commanded*, not requested!"

"Not necessarily." His eyes played over her thoughtfully, and she found herself remembering an oblong of moonlight and the intimate, rocking motion of a sailboat. That night he had neither commanded nor requested. The desire had risen from within both of them, a mutual wellspring of want and need. And why, oh why, was she thinking of that *now?*"

Jan refused to acknowledge what both of them were thinking by anything more than the uncontrollable tinge of color that rose to her face. "Of course. How could I have forgotten? Sometimes you resort to deception instead of direct command," she taunted.

Ignoring the barb, he sat down on one corner of the desk, one foot on the floor, the other dangling lightly. "I was hoping that you wouldn't recognize Anton Bertanoli the other night."

"Yes, it did make for a rather awkward situation, didn't it? But how was I to know Mr. Bertanoli was someone to whom you had already related some amusing tale about our little escapades in Bakersfield . . . and elsewhere?"

"I didn't—"

"Bertanoli recognized my name! He looked at me as if I had a *for sale* sign hung around my neck. You can't possibly deny that you discussed me with him!" Logan said nothing. "Do you deny it?" she demanded.

"No." The large, heavy metal paperclip in Logan's fingers straightened to a jagged line as he bent it effortlessly. "The favor I have to ask is that you not reveal to anyone that Anton is staying at my home." The ruined clip landed with a metallic twang on top the bits of torn check in the wastebasket.

The totally unexpected request momentarily startled Jan out of her fury and scorn. "Why?"

Logan hesitated, as if reluctant to explain. "Anton was in a car accident awhile back. A rather minor accident, actually, but, in one of those ironic twists of fate, it injured a part of him that affected him far more deeply than it might have someone else."

"His right hand?" Jan guessed.

Logan nodded. "He's had surgery on it. Twice. Once at the time of the accident, and then again later. The surgery was considered successful. The doctors put the muscles, tendons, bones, and nerves back in place. But, as Anton says, somehow they couldn't reattach the talent. All of the paintings at the exhibit were done before the accident."

"Oh. I'm so sorry. I realized something was wrong with his hand or arm, but I didn't realize . . ." Jan shook her head helplessly. She was reminded suddenly of her brother's al-most-suicidal despair when he realized he'd be in a wheel-chair for life. He would never water-ski again, never play basketball or tinker around on a junk car. "He must be going through a very difficult time," she said quietly.

Logan nodded again. "Yes. His problems are emotional and psychological as well as physical. But he's coming out of it, and he's starting to paint again. With his left hand!" Jan felt the excitement that progress generated in Logan, and it stirred her, too. "But he's very unsure of himself yet, and he still has some terrible bouts of depression. No one knows he's at the house, so he can work when and how he pleases, at his own speed, with no pressure. But he's suf-ficiently well known that his privacy won't last long if information about his whereabouts gets out."

"He's an old friend?" Jan asked.

"Yes. He was married to my cousin. She and their little boy were killed several years ago in a house fire. Their deaths nearly killed Anton, too, but he buried himself in his painting and managed to survive. And then he had this accident with his hand." Logan's voice was controlled, but Jan sensed an anger in him, a frustrated rage at all that had happened. "But he's improving, both mentally and physi-cally, and he's going to make it if he just has the time and space without outside interference or pressures."

Jan didn't know she had reached for Logan's hand until she felt the warm skin against her fingers. His brief expla-nation had obviously touched only the edges of his concern for his dead cousin's husband. "I won't tell anyone he's at your home. I promise."

His hand turned to clasp hers, his thumb moving in a circular caress over the pulse point on her wrist. She doubted he was even aware of the caress. His thoughts were still on Anton Bertanoli's problems. But she was achingly aware of the absentmindedly sensuous touch and the sweet, silent fire that throbbed up her arm with each pulse beat.

He looked down, suddenly seeming to realize that he was holding her hand. He shifted his weight on the edge of the desk, and suddenly she found herself caught between his outstretched legs, a sinewy thigh on either side of her. His hands slid around the neat curve of her bottom and deftly molded her against him.

She felt a charged rush that wasn't totally the outraged indignation that came out in her explosive, "Logan!"

"Sorry. I almost forgot. We're here to discuss business." He grinned quite unapologetically, an unexpectedly mischievous smile that was at odds with the dignified suit and executive-office setting. "You'd like to work for the station. Tell me about this women's show you have in mind."

He seemed perfectly agreeable to carrying on the interview with her intimately centered between his legs, but she disentangled herself carefully, if for no other reason than that she doubted she could think clearly in that position. She had a warm, disheveled feeling, even though a surreptitious self-inspection detected nothing vital out of place.

Briefly, from a safe half-dozen steps away, she explained the show she and Warren Anderson had discussed. It would start with a short segment of state, national, or even world news of special interest to women, then go on to interviews and issues of local concern. She envisioned both live in-studio shows and videotaped shows of people or events outside the studio. She wanted some programs to show people actually doing things, she emphasized, to avoid a daily diet of talky interviews.

"Perhaps an original play put on by a local theater group," she offered. "Perhaps going into various workplaces and showing women doing their jobs. And some shows with recipes and household ideas because homemaking is an important occupation, too."

Logan listened without comment until she more or less ran down.

"I suppose this isn't actually a—a unique concept," she said finally, a little uncomfortable under his noncommittal gaze. "But I think I can create an interesting and entertaining program."

His expression was still so unrevealing that she was shocked when he said casually, "Sounds like a workable plan to me. We'll give it a try."

Jan had expected to have to argue and defend the idea, and the unexpected capitulation flustered her. "Well, that— that's marvelous! I'm so pleased."

"There's just one problem. We already have a woman on the staff who is qualified and eager to do a show like this. She's had camera experience, and she knows—"

"Stephanie Trainer!" Jan gasped.

"You've met?" Logan's surprise sounded genuine.

"More or less." So that was it—the explanation for Stephanie Trainer's hostility. Stephanie had hoped to snag the midday show for herself! Jan took a deep, steadying breath, willing herself to remain calm and hold back the torrent of indignation she felt at Stephanie's underhanded methods. "I'm sure Miss Trainer is qualified and"— Jan's teeth gritted so hard that they hurt—"and eager, but I believe I have the experience and creative judgement to do a superior job with the show. In addition, I have some ideas about approaching advertisers who don't normally advertise on programs specifically aimed at women."

"Miss Trainer has some ideas of her own, of course. And she does have a university degree in journalism." Almost carelessly, Logan picked up a sheet of paper from the desk. "Ah, but I see you also have a degree. In communications."

Jan suddenly felt impaled, helplessly writhing on the lance of her own lie. She had forgotten all about that incriminating application form. Logan knew her claim to a degree was phony, of course. She had told him she had none.

Damn him, *damn* him, she thought furiously. He'd tricked her, gotten her off guard with his care and concern for Anton Bertanoli and his problems. Like a perfect fool, she'd gone all soft and sympathetic and let her guard down. And all the time he'd had this in reserve, waiting to pounce on her with it. His expression was pleasantly quizzical, but she saw a certain gleam in his eyes. Triumph? Satisfaction? Pure devilish taunt?

"Very well," she said unsteadily. "We both know my claim to a university degree stretched the truth."

"Stretched?" He repeated the word with a lazy, skeptical drawl. "With an understatement like that, perhaps you belong in politics rather than television."

Jan ignored the jibe. "I really don't think a degree is particularly important in this situation," she said carefully. "I believe my experience on the Adele Meeker show in Phoenix speaks for itself."

"Yes, of course. Your experience." He studied the application form. "Let's see . . . you say here you helped write scripts, select and interview guests, edit videotaped shows. Odd," he mused. "I don't see a word here about your job title. 'Glorified Gofer,' wasn't it? And perhaps you forgot to mention *all* your responsibilities, such as pinning up Mrs. Meeker's hem?"

Jan's guilty nervousness erupted into a blaze of anger. "That isn't fair!" she gasped. "You're taking confidential information I told you in—in private, and using it against me. Information you obtained under false pretenses!"

She had never felt more vulnerably exposed. Their eyes locked, his narrowed thoughtfully, hers wide and dark with anger and dismay. He knew all her fears and weaknesses, knew exactly where to jab a sensitive spot or probe a vulnerable area.

His eyes, leisurely roaming her tense figure, insolently said he knew all that and more. He knew the naked look and feel of her breasts now rising and falling with her agitated breathing. He knew the pressure of her legs twined around his and the ecstatic shudder of her body as they both reached fulfillment.

"The show is my idea," she added thickly. "You have no right to let Stephanie Trainer—"

"As a matter of fact, you'll both have a chance at the show." Suddenly the briskly professional executive, he went around behind the desk and sat down in the swivel chair. "We've decided to start out with a twice-weekly show.

Tuesdays and Thursdays. You'll have one show. Stephanie will do the other."

"That still isn't fair," Jan said hotly. "You're cutting her in on my—"

"If it weren't for me, Stephanie would have the entire show. That was what Bruce Gurley planned to do."

Jan's mouth formed a small, startled "Oh!"

"Later, after we see how the show goes, it may be expanded to five days a week. At that time, one of you could emerge as permanent hostess. Or, if you could manage to set personal antagonisms aside, a co-hostess arrangement might be more interesting."

"Possibly." Jan's agreement was guarded.

"In the meantime, you'll be expected to handle some other duties around the station. I'm sure you realize that, at a small station such as this, everyone does a bit of everything. On your show, you and Stephanie will be working with Hank Rossland, who produces the local news shows. Your duties and responsibilities for the show will be of considerably wider scope than they would be at a larger station. You'll be expected to handle most details yourselves." He fixed her with a steady gaze. "Are you interested?"

"Yes, of course!" Except for having to share the show with Stephanie, this was exactly what Jan wanted. She'd have a real opportunity to learn everything. "When do I start?"

"Monday morning." He flicked through some other papers. "Your salary and fringe benefits will be the same as you had discussed with Warren Anderson."

"Thank you."

Logan picked up her application form, studied it for a long moment, then deliberately crumpled it into a wrinkled ball and tossed it into the wastebasket.

Jan hesitated, feeling a twisted tightness in her stomach slowly loosen. She was grateful that he had destroyed her lie, yet she hated the sudden realization that she was now in his debt. "Thank you," she repeated stiffly.

"A less ethical boss might demand some—ah—more

specific show of gratitude," he suggested. The dancing deviltry was in his eyes again. "Something more on the physical side."

"But you're not that type."

He sighed regretfully. "No."

Jan moved toward the door before she lost ground in this
small verbal sparring match. "I'll be here Monday morning."

He stood up and followed her to the door. "Remember
your promise," he said.

Promise? Her heart gave an inexplicable lurch before she
remembered the promise was nothing personal, just her
agreement not to mention Anton Bertanoli's whereabouts
to anyone. She nodded.

"And, Jan . . ."

"Yes?" Her heart galloped wildly.

"I know why you filled out the application form as you
did. But it wasn't exactly ethical." His voice held a hint of
veiled warning.

"I know, and I'm sorry."

Those final moments sobered Jan but couldn't dull her
excitement. The show wasn't all she had originally hoped
for, but it was a start. And if the show did go daily, she
vowed then and there that she would be the one chosen as
permanent hostess. How much contact would she have with
Logan at the station? Probably very little. Yet she knew that
some small part of her excitement—perhaps not such a
small part of it, she had to admit reluctantly—came from
the prospect of working with him for a while.

Jan wished she could have started work the very next
day. The time until Monday seemed endless. Unexpectedly,
something happened to fill Friday and Saturday. A co-
worker of Shelley's had been leaving her three-year-old
daughter at what she thought was a reputable day-care center. She was a single mother, working frantically at Buenaventura Development on weekdays and at a second job on
Saturdays to make ends meet. Now the authorities had
abruptly closed the child-care facility on a number of
charges, not the least of which were both licensing and

zoning violations. The woman was desperate to find some-one to take care of her little girl, and Jan offered to help out.

It was an enjoyable and enlightening two days for Jan in several ways. She hadn't baby-sat since high school, and she had almost forgotten how much she enjoyed toddlers. She also learned a great deal in a very short time about the problems working women encountered finding reliable, quality child care. Susan Norris had a handful of small horror stories to tell about her experiences.

Jan planned Sunday as a lazy, do-nothing day, but the weather was so deliciously springlike that staying inside seemed a shame. She had just decided to drive down to the beach and go for a walk when the telephone rang.

"Am I interrupting anything?" Logan asked without pre-liminaries.

"No."

"It occurred to me after I dialed that Paul might have stayed the night."

"No!" She nibbled her lower lip, realizing she hadn't told Logan about her breakup with Paul, if ending such a briefly resumed relationship could be termed a breakup. Not that it was any of Logan's business anyway, she thought with a certain belligerence. She still hated to admit to Logan that his quick assessment of Paul had been absolutely right.

"I'm down at the marina," he continued. "I thought I'd take the sailboat out for a while. Would you like to come along?" He made the invitation sound like a challenge.

"Does this come under the heading of showing specific gratitude to the boss?" she retorted.

"I'm not your boss until Monday," he pointed out. "However, you're welcome to make any displays of grati-tude you think...ummm...appropriate." She heard husky laughter in his voice.

Damn him, she thought, but without the rancor she'd felt during their interview. Just when she was trying to put him down with some cutting remark, he made her feel like laughing instead. "I'll bring lunch," she offered.

"If that's the limit of your gratitude, I suppose I'll have

to settle for it." He sighed. "Half an hour?"

"Half an hour," she agreed, and suddenly the day had a new and delightful zest.

She threw together a lunch of leftover cold chicken, French bread, an assortment of crunchy vegetable sticks and cherry tomatoes, tortilla chips, cheese, and fruit for dessert. After only a moment's hesitation, she appropriated Shelley's unopened bottle of white wine. Shelley's fiancé preferred beer anyway, though Shelley was still trying to win him over to what she considered a more sophisticated drink.

Logan was tinkering with the auxiliary engine when Jan arrived. He was wearing jeans and an old sweatshirt. This one had sleeves intact, though otherwise it was as disreputable-looking as the one he'd worn on their previous date. Here on the water there was the usual breeze, and his hair was wind-tousled around the sunglasses pushed back on his head. Jan was struck again by the male-animal vigor that evoked something vibrantly female within her, like a shivery tingle, only deeper. Much deeper. His glance approved her slim-fitting jeans and cotton blouse knotted under her breasts. But her long hair was already flying around her face. She should have worn a scarf.

He stowed the lunch and her sweater in the cabin and stepped out to the cockpit carrying a short length of yellow cord. "Turn around."

Jan turned obediently. He caught her flying hair and smoothed it back from her face with strokes that Jan tried to tell herself were efficient rather than sensual. He tied her hair in a practical ponytail at the nape of her neck with the cord. Jan held herself very still, willing herself not to react as his fingers whispered over her hair. Keep this light, breezy, and casual, she warned herself. But she couldn't escape another shivery tingle when his fingers brushed her neck.

"Cold?"

"No, just excited. I've never been sailing before," she explained quickly, so he wouldn't misinterpret. She was all too aware of the proximity of the cabin and bed where they had made love. From the knowing smile on his mouth, she suspected her quick explanation was wasted. He knew exactly what she found exciting. And it wasn't just sailing for the first time.

Within moments, however, Jan discovered that sailing *was* exciting. Logan used the engine to maneuver the boat through the spiky forest of sailboat masts, then out between the rock jetties that protected the harbor entrance. She stayed out of the way in the cockpit while he unfurled the sails. There was something invigorating about seeing the blue and white sails catch the breeze and billow gently, a fine, glorious feeling of freedom as the little boat swept along under nature's free power.

"Are we going out to the islands?" Jan asked.

"Not today." Logan skillfully adjusted the sail at just the right angle to send the boat skimming parallel to the shoreline, which already seemed a surprising distance away. "We should have at least a full day to sail out and explore the islands."

Did that mean he thought they'd be seeing more of each other? Or was the "we" just an expression of speech? Jan felt an unexpected pang as she suddenly realized that his last-minute invitation to come along today quite possibly meant he'd originally planned to bring some other girl and had called Jan only when the other plans fell through for some reason.

The thought disturbed her for a moment. Then she flung it to the breeze. Her loss, my gain! she thought recklessly, turning her face to the sun and wind. She felt an almost unreasonable joy as she looked up at Logan's lithely powerful body silhouetted against the blue sky. He grinned down at her, his legs spread to balance himself as he braced one arm against the mast.

"Enjoying yourself?" he called.

"Yes. It's marvelous! Let's sail 'round the world!"

He flashed her another pirate grin, and she had the giddy feeling that with Logan sailing 'round the world wasn't at all out of the realm of possibility. With Logan, anything was possible!

From here the town looked lush and green, with here

and there a flash of white walls or red tile roof, though farther back the subdivisions marched inexorably up the bare hills that were still faintly greenish at this time of year. Away from town, she could see the line of Highway 101 edging the coastline, and now and then sunlight caught a windshield with a brilliant flash. Other sail and motor boats skimmed the water, and the occupants exchanged friendly waves. Logan told her it was also possible at this time of year to see the great gray whales on their annual migration, and once she caught a strange, rolling motion that might have been caused by one of the enormous creatures.

They put in at a little cove with a crescent of sand enclosed by rock ridges at either end. The highway was visible, but it was as inaccessible over the rocks as if it were on another planet. Logan went first, then offered Jan a hand to make the leap from bobbing boat to rocks. The cove was sheltered from the wind and pleasantly warm and sunny. The lunch Jan had prepared didn't call for a fire, but the lovely seclusion and abundance of driftwood did.

They gathered bits of wood and got a fragrant blaze going. Logan went back to the boat and returned with their lunch, a battered tin coffeepot, and a blanket. Jan spread out the lunch while Logan made a nest at the edge of the fire for the coffeepot.

They fell on the food with indelicate gusto. Jan was unexpectedly ravenous. The coffee promptly boiled over and came out strong and bitter, but it tasted delicious anyway. Their conversation was limited to practical bits of exchange.

"More chicken?" she inquired.

"Please."

"What happened to the taco chips?" She peered into the sack.

"I ate them all."

"Glutton."

When they got to the cheese and fruit, Jan opened the wine. It was the supermarket's next-to-cheapest brand, but it, too, tasted glorious. Jan lay back on the blanket, balancing the styrofoam cup of wine on her bare midriff. Her feelings were a happy blend of sated hunger, peace, and relaxation.

"So, how goes the conquest of Paul?" Logan inquired. He had removed his sweatshirt and lay barechested on his side, his head braced by a bent arm.

"You make me sound as if I'm some sort of big-game trophy hunter," Jan objected.

"Are·you?"

"I'm not seeing Paul again." She paused only momentarily before adding, "He turned out to be everything you thought he was." Unexpectedly, the admission didn't turn out to be particularly difficult to say after all. Paul seemed long ago, a vague memory. "Are you going to say, 'I told you so'?"

"I'll try to restrain myself." He took a lazy sip of wine, and Jan appreciated that he didn't seem skeptical or ask for explanations or details, that he simply accepted what she said. "So, what have you been doing with yourself? Besides storming out to Ojai to—to interview for a job?" The slight pause in mid-sentence sounded as if he had a sudden change of mind and decided not to mention her hostile visit to his house.

Jan felt a stirring of remembered anger. For all his distracting charm, he *had* "kissed and told," to put it mildly. She mustn't let her guard down too far. He wasn't to be trusted. He wasn't above using anything she told him against her, she reminded herself sternly.

But it was hard to remember those warnings here on the sun-warmed beach, with the gentle swish of the surf and the crackle of the fire in her ears, and a disturbing awareness of Logan lying next to her on the blanket. He had slid closer and now he used her bare midriff as a shelf for his own cup of wine. His hand rested with easy intimacy on her bare skin.

"I spent Friday and Saturday taking care of the three-year-old daughter of a friend of my roommate's. She was having baby-sitter problems. We baked peanut butter cookies and invited the neighbor's cat in for a visit and drew about five thousand pictures." Jan chuckled, remembering little Beth's insatiable demand for pictures. She had a surprising ability of her own to capture essentials with rough stick figures.

"You sound as if you enjoyed the experience." Logan's thumb traced a circular path around her navel. Something deeper, as if connected by previously unknown nerve paths, reacted with a small, yearning spasm. "What about children of your own? Or does a television career come first? How ambitious are you?"

Jan didn't answer immediately. So far this wasn't a problem she'd had to wrestle with intimately, but she had considered it, of course. She swirled her cup of wine reflectively. A shift in the breeze brought the distant sound of traffic from the highway, but it was muted and not unpleasant. "Ideally, I suppose I'd like to establish myself in television first, then combine a career and motherhood. And do a superb job of both, of course." She laughed ruefully. "But I'm not sure that's possible. I suppose I'm old-fashioned enough to believe that, once a woman actually has children, they have to come first. At least, for a while."

"A husband and father for those children belongs in there somewhere too," Logan suggested. Prowling fingertips dipped beneath the snug snap of her jeans to explore the flat plane of her abdomen.

Talking about children with Logan suddenly seemed too intimate, almost painfully so, and his touch was distracting. Deliberately she came back with a lightly teasing retort to change the mood. "Well, if science keeps making all these marvelous leaps forward in technology, women won't need men to . . ."

Logan lifted his styrofoam cup and deliberately trickled a few drops of wine into the hollow of her navel. "So much for the marvelous leaps of science," he growled. "Some things will always be better the old-fashioned way."

Jan's knees automatically came up when the chilled liquid hit her skin, and the wine overflowed in a cold trickle down her side. With a deft flick of his tongue, Logan lapped it up. Jan laughed, but it was a breathless little laugh, and she quickly rolled over on her stomach to halt the flurry of delicious little shivers that exploded around the touch of his tongue.

She asked quickly, "Do you know yet how long you'll be acting as manager at the station?" She buried her fingertips in the warm sand to control their sudden incriminating tremble.

"Nothing more than I told you. Two or three weeks. Do you really want to talk business on a beautiful day like this?"

"It's a good, safe subject."

"Very well, we'll discuss business then." He sounded resigned.

He talked about some of the problems with the physical layout of the station. Jan hadn't realized it before, but Logan's company hadn't actually founded the station. They had purchased it when the former company floundered financially before actually getting any programs on the air. Jan noted that he was careful not to make any references to people working at the station. He was obviously well aware of the potential for conflict there.

All the time he talked, sounding very professional and businesslike, his hand made long, delicious strokes over the rounded curve of her derriere. She ought to stop him, she thought dreamily. But she felt more like purring, lulled like a contented cat dozing in the sun.

"I don't think you're listening," Logan chided finally.

He was right. Her thoughts had wandered. "Logan, have you discussed me with anyone other than Anton Bertanoli?" she asked abruptly.

The roaming hand paused on the rounded curve of her snugly filled jeans. "I discussed hiring you with Bruce Gurley and Hank Rossland." He sounded wary.

"You know that isn't what I mean."

"No." The word was curt, half-angry. "I haven't discussed you with anyone other than Anton."

"He must have gotten a big laugh out of my mistake. Did you tell him...everything?"

"I told him everything I thought was pertinent."

"But you didn't tell anyone else?"

"No."

At least she wasn't the topic of some risqué story making the cocktail-party circuit, she thought, partly relieved. He rolled away from her and lay flat on his back, one arm flung across his eyes. His solid rib cage sloped down to his flat abdomen with an intriguing line of fine hair that glinted gold against the deep tan. He was angry with her. She felt a small flare of resentment. What right had *he* to be angry? He was the one who had "kissed and told." Even if Logan himself told no one else, Anton Bertanoli might think it an entertaining story to pass on. Yes, she had every right to be angry at his deception.

But in spite of her anger and resentment, she felt an almost irresistible urge to slide her palm across the sun-warmed plateau of his stomach, comb her fingertips through the fine curl of chest hair . . .

Instead, with a kind of wild glee, she grabbed the bottle of wine and dumped the pale liquid indiscriminately from navel to throat, relishing his yelp of indignation.

"What the hell do you think you're doing?"

He yanked the bottle out of her hand and planted it in the sand. Jan saw the determined gleam in his eyes and scrambled across the blanket in hasty retreat, but she was too slow. One powerful hand caught her around the ankle, and a moment later she was trapped under his body, her blouse bunched up so that only the honey-colored lace of her bra separated her tingling breasts from his naked chest.

"You did it to me!" she protested. "I was just paying you back."

"I dribbled a couple of tiny little drops on you. Like this." His tongue made a small darting flick against her lips, like a series of dancing drops of wine. "And you gave me a damned bath in the stuff. Like *this.*" His mouth came down hard on hers, an all-encompassing, overflowing kiss that filled her mouth with the powerful probe of his tongue. She could smother in the kiss, she thought, drown in it . . . and she didn't object to the idea at all. When he finally lifted his mouth, her heart was thundering.

"There, you see what happens to girls who misbehave?

If I let you up, do you think you can behave now?"

"I don't think so." Her tone was tremulous.

He shifted his weight and dipped his head to nudge the sheer wisp of bra aside. His tongue could reach just far enough to barely tantalize the sensitive tip of her breast, and she made a small, writhing movement of frustration, wanting more than that tantalizing flick.

With sudden inspiration, her hands slid up and unfastened the front closing of the bra. He raised up and with one hand gently pushed the sheer material aside until her breasts were nakedly exposed to the warmth of sun and kiss of breeze...and the even sweeter warmth of his gaze and caress of his lips. His tongue traced the dividing line left by her bathing suit, where honey-tan skin met creamy white.

She drifted with the heady feeling, caught between the sand beneath her hollowed to the shape of her body and the hard length of his body contoured above her. The tangy scent of the ocean blended with the smoky-sweet fragrance of the fire and a certain indefinable scent of maleness about him. No, not a scent; it was too faint for that. An aura...an aura that stirred her senses and roused moonlight memories. But when his hand slid to the snap of her jeans, she stopped him.

"Not here!" she gasped, blinking into the sunlight.

"Didn't I tell you once that you were missing something if you made love only hidden in darkness?" His whisper was a caress against her ear.

"But there are cars up there...and people in them!" She clutched frantically at the blouse as she saw a car stop at a lookout point behind a guard rail. "I don't like an audience!"

He laughed lazily. "I take it you're not the type who intends to bare her all for the camera someday?"

"No!" Jan tried to stuff her dangling bra inside the blouse, but without much success.

"Good." His deft hands opened the blouse, cupped the sheer material of the bra around her breasts, and fastened the closing. He continued until the blouse was buttoned and neatly knotted again. "There. All back in order."

"Thank you." Her voice was unsteady.

He leaned over and brushed her lips lightly with his. "I meant what I said," he warned softly. "And this time I intend to see your eyes when I make love to you."

"You're taking a lot for granted, aren't you?" she retorted. She started gathering up the scattered lunch items.

He just smiled lazily. They both knew that this golden, delicious day could have only one possible ending.

CHAPTER

Eight

THE AIR HAD chilled considerably by the time the sailboat
glided back into the boat slip at the marina. A cold fog bank
was moving in from the islands, and the marina was busy
with returning boats. The sounds of engines and voices
mingled with the shrieks of gulls and the other, never quite
indentifiable, bongs and musical tinkles that were a part of
the marina background. The cold, depressing fog sliding in
had no effect on Jan. She had a heady something-wonderful-
is-going-to-happen feeling, and she had only to look at Logan's slow smile to know she was right.

Jan carried the remains of their lunch and the empty wine
bottle to a trash barrel while Logan finished making the boat
secure for the night.

"Do you want to eat somewhere in town or go out to the

house?" Logan called as she jumped lightly from boat to concrete dock.

"Whatever you want—" Jan broke off. A tall, dark-haired woman in white slacks had stopped in mid-stride to look at her, lips parted in astonishment. "Hello, Stephanie." Jan clutched her paper sack of garbage, feeling uncomfortable under the woman's shocked gaze. "Have you been sailing?"

Stephanie waved her hand vaguely toward a sailboat moored several slips away. It was larger than Logan's boat, elegant with teak deck and brass fittings. "My parents keep their boat here. We went out for a while." She was staring at the back of Logan's head as he adjusted something on the engine.

"Beautiful day, wasn't it?" Jan intended to edge past the other woman, but Stephanie fell into step beside her.

"I didn't know you were a personal friend of Logan Pierce's. Have you known him long?"

"Not long," Jan answered noncommittally. "I hear you and I are going to be working together."

"More or less."

They had reached the trash barrel, and Jan jammed the paper sack and bottle inside. She turned and started back toward the boat. Stephanie moved with her, as if some invisible leash joined them.

"Did you know Logan before he interviewed you at the station last week?" Stephanie persisted.

Jan pushed back a lock of mist-dampened hair that had escaped from the ponytail. "I really don't think that's any of your—"

"You *did* know him, didn't you?" A triumphant realization-is-dawning glitter shone in Stephanie's dark eyes. "So that's why he insisted on hiring you! Bruce—Mr. Gurley said he made a real issue of it."

"I was assured of a job by Warren Anderson before his death. Mr. Pierce was simply carrying out a commitment that had already been made to me." Jan spoke stiffly, unhappily aware that Stephanie had undoubtedly examined the application form rather carefully. Would the lie about the college degree come back to haunt Jan again? "My experience qualified me—"

"Experience!" Stephanie gave an unladylike snort. "I'm sure experience is exactly the reason you got the job. That and various talents more evident in a bedroom than a television station!"

Jan's thoughts had been fastened on the incriminating misstatement she had made on the application form, and it took a moment for Stephanie's insulting words to sink in. Jan stopped short as she realized that a university degree was hardly the issue. The shock was on *her* face now.

"So what did you decide?" Stephanie's voice, which sounded so warm and rich over the air, now held a malicious taunt.

Jan momentarily floundered in confusion. Stephanie obviously knew she had accepted the job. "Decide about what?"

"About dinner. Did you decide on downtown or something more . . . ummm . . . intimate at Logan's house? It does help to be sleeping with the boss when you're out to get a job, doesn't it?"

With a disdainful glance, Stephanie turned on her heel and stalked with long-legged strides toward the parking lot. Jan just stood there, too shocked to move. Not even a tardy putdown came to mind. What *could* she say? She wasn't exactly involved in a full-blown affair with Logan, but they had made love once. And undoubtedly they would again tonight.

She jerked as a companionable arm circled her shoulders. "Were you talking to someone?"

"Just a—girl."

"The boat is all taken care of, so we're ready to leave."

Jan's feet moved automatically, but her thoughts raced and tumbled headlong. Logic told her that Stephanie was just guessing with her crude "sleeping with the boss" accusation. She couldn't know for certain that the relationship had gone beyond an innocent sailing afternoon. But the brutal fact was that the relationship wasn't exactly innocent. It was an intimate one, and perhaps she *had* gotten the job not because of any television abilities but because of her prowess in bed!

The thought made Jan feel angry and disgusted and a little ill. There couldn't be anything to it! Stephanie just had an ugly and suspicious mind. Jan had always abhorred women who used sex to get ahead in their careers. Logan had hired her because she had the ability and qualifications for the job—hadn't he? But would he, some small, sly voice asked, have been so quick to overlook that lie about her education if they hadn't made love together? Would she even have gotten in to see him for an interview, let alone been offered a job at the station?

They reached the parking lot. Jan's car, blurred in the drifting mist, was on the far side from Logan's Ferrari.

"What did you decide about dinner?" he asked.

"I—I'm really not hungry. I think I'll just go straight home."

"What?" Logan looked and sounded incredulous.

"So I'll see you tomorrow," she said. She edged toward the curb, her chin tilted defiantly. "At the station."

His sudden grip on her upper arm stopped her. "What's going on? I thought—" He broke off, his tanned forehead slashed with scowl lines. "You seem to change your mind the way some people do TV stations. What is it this time?"

"What makes you think there was any change of mind?" Jan retorted. "If you thought I was interested in anything more than a—sailboat ride, perhaps you jumped to conclusions you shouldn't have."

He dropped her arm and stared at her, half-puzzled, half-angry. She thought momentarily of demanding to know why he had hired her. But he would hardly admit something crude, such as, "Because I like the way you perform in bed." He'd say what he thought she wanted to hear, and then rush her out to his house—and bedroom.

"You're serious?" He still sounded disbelieving.

"Quite serious." she added bluntly, "I assume this won't affect your job offer?"

Without bothering to reply, he stalked to the Ferrari, leaving Jan to locate her own car in the misty dusk. She

drove home angry and upset. If there was anything to Stephanie's suspicion that Jan had been hired because of her
intimate relationship with Logan, which had now become
Jan's reluctant suspicion also, she was more than ever determined to demonstrate that she could handle the job. She
could not only handle it but also prove that her talents and
abilities were superior to Stephanie Trainer's!

Jan arrived at the station Monday morning feeling as if
she were walking onto a battlefield. The feeling did not
improve when Linda, the receptionist, showed her into a
conference room where a meeting on the new show had
already been scheduled. Logan hadn't arrived yet, and the
only people Jan recognized sitting at the rectangular table
were Stephanie Trainer and Bruce Gurley. Neither of them
rushed to welcome her. Jan took a seat and studied her notes
nervously. She felt a surge of relief when Logan strode in
and took his place at the head of the table. But the relief
was short-lived. He gave her neither a word nor a glance
of encouragement, merely introduced her to the others at
the table.

And that was the way it should be, the way she wanted
it, Jan reminded herself resolutely. The last thing she wanted
was any favortism from Logan.

She tried to keep names and faces straight. Bruce Gurley
and Stephanie were no problem, of course. The beefy man
with turned-back shirt cuffs was Hank Rossland, the news
producer-director with whom she'd be working directly.
Two men from the sales department were there, plus the
promotion manager and several others whose names and
titles escaped Jan.

Jan was called on first to give her views and ideas on
the program. She was aware of Stephanie's chafing impatiently for her to finish so she could insert her own ideas.
Bruce Gurley, who seemed more interested in doodling on
his blank notepad than in Jan's presentation, listened attentively and nodded affirmatively while Stephanie spoke.
Hank Rossland looked harried, and Jan suspected that he
wasn't any too happy to have the responsibilities of another
show. He'd be pleased, Jan further suspected shrewdly, to

let her and Stephanie take on as much responsibility for the program as they cared to.

Jan was glad to see that no one seemed to have rigid, preconceived ideas about what subjects or formats were suitable for the show. The field appeared to be wide open. Jan said she'd like to do her first show on the problems working women encountered finding quality day care for their children. The idea was approved, with only a minor disparaging note from Bruce Gurley. Jan made more points when she offered her suggestions about reaching advertisers who normally avoided women-oriented shows.

Then Stephanie, sounding uncharacteristically modest, said she had a suggestion for the opening show. Stephanie had attended college with and was a personal friend of a young woman named Susan Welch. They had, in fact, worked together in several college dramas, Stephanie added in that same deceptively modest tone. The name made no impression on Jan but several people recognized Susan Welch as an actress who played a starring role in what was currently the hottest soap opera on daytime television. A stirring of interest circled the table.

"Do you think you might get her to appear on the show?" Bruce Gurley asked. Jan instantly realized it was a prearranged line. Stephanie and Bruce had this all planned.

"I can do better than that. Susan has been dating both her leading men on the show. There's been a lot of speculation about which one she might marry." With a triumphant look at Jan, Stephanie dropped her blockbuster. "She says she'll come on *my* show and announce her forthcoming marriage to one of the men."

"Wow! Think of the publicity we can generate with that!" the promotion manager exclaimed. He actually looked a little awed.

With a sinking feeling, Jan realized that Stephanie had been holding this news back until just the proper moment to top any and everything Jan had offered. And it had certainly worked. Stephanie got the lead-off show, of course, and the remainder of the meeting was devoted to how best to exploit the publicity value of this unexpected plum.

The competition, Jan realized grimly as the meeting finally broke for a late lunch, was going to be a lot more keen than she had anticipated. However, she suspected that Stephanie might not really be in any position to throw rocks at the glass walls of Jan's brief involvement with Logan. Something was going on between Bruce Gurley and Stephanie. And Bruce was married.

The next two weeks before the show was scheduled to go on the air were hectic. Jan ignored the hoopla and publicity about the first show with the soap-opera star and her big announcement, though it rankled every time the spot ads ended with, "Watch Stephanie Trainer's new show, *Women's View,* starting Tuesday!"

Jan concentrated on making her first show the best possible. Most of it had to be videotaped outside the studio, and sometimes Jan felt like the unloved stepchild of the show as she had to wait or scheme for a videotaping crew. The woman for whom she had baby-sat put her in touch with various other women with child-care problems. Jan worked right through the weekend, talking to women who weren't available at other times.

However, her busy schedule did not prevent her from noticing that Logan was ignoring her. As she had assumed, she actually saw very little of him around the station. When she did run into him, he was correct and formal.

Stephanie's first show came off with much fanfare. Some of the suspense was dissipated when the soap-opera star's decision leaked out ahead of time, but it was still a very successful launch show. Stephanie made no direct accusations, but Jan knew Stephanie suspected that the leak had come from Jan. Jan herself suspected that the soap-opera star's publicity agent had something to do with it.

Jan's first show seemed rather prosaic and workaday after Stephanie's razzle-dazzle, but she was gratified by the personal response it drew. She received numerous phone calls from women who had simply given up trying to work because of child-care problems. She got one call from a man who said that this was more than a working woman's problem. As a divorced father who had custody of his children, he had the same difficulty finding reliable help. Jan saw the makings of another show there. Altogether, she felt very good about her first show, but of course it was Stephanie who got her picture in the paper with the soap-opera star.

The new station manager arrived the following Monday. Logan let Gordon Palmer take over immediately and didn't hang around to tell him how to do his job. Logan's immediate exit seemed to emphasize the fact that the television station was only one of many interests in which Logan's company was involved, and probably a rather minor one at that. Mr. Palmer seemed capable and efficient, thorough rather than flashy. Jan believed she could expect equitable treatment from him.

She was acutely aware, however, that with Logan no longer at the station to keep an eye on them, Stephanie and Bruce Gurley considered her fair game. Jan suspected they thought she spent half her nights frolicking in Logan's hot tub and bed. Little did they know, she thought ruefully. Jan and Logan hardly spoke to each other, let alone frolicked.

Jan carefully hid the empty ache she felt when Logan was no longer at the station. Even if she had rarely seen, and even more rarely talked to him, she enjoyed a stimulating feeling of anticipation in knowing he was nearby. She always felt a little tingle of excitement when she walked past his door. There was always the tantalizing possibility that something *could* happen between them. And now that possibility was gone.

Still, the job was exciting, and Jan tried to content herself with that. In addition to her weekly Thursday show, she did a variety of other jobs, from last-minute news writing to supplying the voice-over for a waterbed commercial. She had always heard that working on a small local station was the best way to learn all aspects of television, and she believed it.

Jan's second show, which focused on a natural-birth-control method, aroused some controversy among viewers, but also stimulated interest. All Stephanie's energies seemed to have gone into her first show, and her second was a limp interview with a very dull writer of genealogical articles. However, Jan felt no sense of satisfaction with Stephanie's lackluster show. She was aware that *every* show must be interesting if they were to enlarge their viewing audience.

Jan did a little surreptitious checking on Stephanie, thinking it never hurt to know all she could about a working partner—or adversary. Most of what she found out came from Linda, the receptionist. Linda said that Stephanie came from a wealthy, locally socially prominent family. After graduating from college, Stephanie had spent about a year back east in a nontelevision job, then returned here so she could get into television.

"She's ambitious. *Very* ambitious," Linda warned. "So watch out for her. She's pretty thick with Bruce Gurley, as you may have noticed."

It was odd that a girl with Stephanie's ambitions and methods hadn't tried to get somewhere with Logan, Jan mused to herself.

As if reading her thoughts, Linda added in an even more confidential tone, "She made a play for Logan Pierce when he first showed up here, but he just ignored her. Miss High-and-Mighty Trainer was *not* pleased."

Another reason for Stephanie's hostility, Jan realized. She did not intend to ignore Linda's warnings about Stephanie's ambition.

Jan held a small hope that once Logan was through at the station he might contact her, but the first Saturday passed in silence. She toyed with the idea of calling him and casually suggesting a hike or picnic. Finally, however, on Sunday afternoon she settled for a small, female artifice of which she was not particularly proud—going where she thought he might be and hoping she might "accidentally" run into him.

She was surprised and a little uncomfortable when the small scheme actually worked. She drove to the marina, wandered with forced casualness out toward the boats, and there he was, barechested, scowling, striding toward her with a gasoline can in one hand and a wrench in the other.

His eyes raked over her, and she had the impression he knew exactly why she was there. So why not admit it? she challenged herself recklessly.

"Hi. I—I thought I might find you here today. It's a beautiful day for sailing."

"Yes, isn't it?" His voice was flat, totally lacking in encouragement.

"I thought if I came down here . . . maybe someone would offer to take me sailing." She smiled tentatively, which was as daring as she could get. Her eyes begged him to make it easier for her, but if he saw the plea, he ignored it.

"If you stroll around, I'm sure you'll get some offers." His eyes deliberately dropped to the full curve of her sherbet-pink T-shirt. At home, the T-shirt had looked neat and trim-fitting; under Logan's roving gaze, it felt as snug as a pink sunburn—and little more substantial.

Jan took a steadying breath. "You're still angry, aren't you?"

"Puzzled might be a better word." He sounded guarded.

"It was just that it suddenly occurred to me that night that with both of us working at the station . . . I mean, I wasn't sure why . . . I wanted to prove . . ." Jan choked over her awkward jumble of words as a middle-aged couple carrying fishing poles strolled by and looked at her curiously. "It's rather awkward discussing this here. If we could talk somewhere else? Perhaps your boat?"

"I'm not alone."

"Oh!" The solid concrete walkway suddenly seemed to tilt crazily. Of course he wasn't alone! Why hadn't that possibility—*probability*—occurred to her? He was *Logan Pierce,* bachelor extraordinaire, and she certainly wasn't the only woman treated to a romp on his sailboat bed! The idea that he had given her a job at the TV station on that basis suddenly seemed preposterous. Willing women were undoubtedly a commodity he had in oversupply. "It—it's been nice talking to you," she stammered inanely, her face a pink reflection of her T-shirt as she turned to flee.

"Jan!"

She tried to keep going, but the commanding voice halted

her in her tracks, as if her muscles were under his control rather than her own. Reluctantly she glanced back over her shoulder. "You're shouting," she muttered.

"Why did you come here today?"

Because I'm falling in love with you. Jan clapped a horrified hand over her mouth, afraid she had spoken the unintended words aloud. They weren't true, she thought wildly . . . or were they?

"It was just an unfortunate impulse," she finally said stiffly. "I didn't intend to interrupt anything intimate." She willed her feet to move on, and clumsily, they obeyed.

"Anton Bertanoli is with me."

"Anton!" Jan repeated, jerking to a halt.

"He has a place of his own now. I thought getting out for a sail might do him good."

"I'm sure it will." Jan felt chagrined but relieved. But the fact was, she *was* intruding. She backed away, murmuring some vague pleasantry.

"So if you'd like to come along . . . ?"

Jan hesitated. "I wouldn't want to intrude." Logan grinned unexpectedly. "I'm sure Anton will appreciate the chance to get to know you better. After all I've told him about you," he mocked lightly.

Jan hesitated again, torn between wanting to be with Logan and knowing how uncomfortable she would feel in Anton Bertanoli's knowing presence. Was Logan unchivalrous enough to have made her sound like some oversexed nymphet in his amusing tales? She suddenly suspected that Logan took a certain perverse pleasure in her discomfort. "I'm sure I'll enjoy getting to know Mr. Bertanoli better, too," she finally said defiantly.

The day was beautifully sunny, but a storm center lay somewhere far out to sea, and the winds in advance of it were tricky. Logan was kept busy adjusting the sails to accommodate the gusty shifts in direction. Jan and Anton sat on benches built into the cockpit, fairly well protected from the breeze. They exchanged a few casual comments about the weather and boat. Jan felt distinctly uncomfortable even though Anton was polite, quite friendly, and made not even the slightest reference to anything Logan had told him.

Jan was curious about how Anton's painting with his left hand was progressing, but she didn't want to ask and perhaps upset him. She filled in a lull by saying, "Logan has a lovely home, doesn't he? And the Ojai Valley is a beautiful area."

"Yes, Very beautiful. I'll never be able to repay Logan for his generosity in letting me stay there during a very difficult time in my life." Anton smiled, a nice flash of white teeth against his naturally dark complexion. "Logan always seems to know when to give me a pep talk and when to nag or sympathize. And when to say nothing at all. He is a most exceptional man. And friend. If I am ever able to paint again, much of the credit must be given to him."

"*If* you paint again? But I thought . . . Aren't you painting now?"

"I use my brushes. I make marks on the canvas. Some kind friends tell me the work is good." He shrugged as if doubting this judgement. He looked down at his right hand. "This hand is useless. The talent did not mend when the bones and muscles did." He spread his left hand and looked at it in disgust. "And this hand never had any talent to begin with."

"But the talent isn't in your hands," Jan argued earnestly. "It is in your head."

"So I am told." He shrugged again, dismissing the statement as meaningless.

"But I know it's true. Let me tell you about my brother." Jan scooted closer. She told him about Mike's accident, his despair, the months when he wouldn't even try to do anything. She never knew what got Mike past that low point, though she strongly suspected it was simply the persistent prayers of people who cared and loved him. But he had come out of it, and step by step he had learned how to cope, learned how to do old things in new ways, and then gone on to new things. "Most people use their feet to operate pedals when they drive a car, right? But Mike has a car specially equipped with hand controls. What I'm trying to say is that the ability—the *talent* to drive, if you want to put it that way—wasn't in his feet. It was in his head. And that's where your talent is."

As she spoke, Jan forgot her uncomfortable self-consciousness with Anton. She even momentarily forgot Logan nearby in her urgent need to communicate what she felt.

"Mike always wanted to be a mechanic, and he is one. He can't crawl all over cars anymore, but he can rebuild generators and alternators, and he's very good at it."

Anton shook his head ruefully. "I'm making such a big fuss over one hand. Your brother had much more to conquer. You make me ashamed of myself."

"Oh, I didn't mean to do that," Jan said contritely. She was aware of Logan's watching them now, a curious expression on his face. "I didn't intend to preach."

Anton laughed. "You make a most beautiful preacher." He cocked his head thoughtfully and then nodded slowly. "But you've made me think, and perhaps I will try something I've been considering." Anton went on to explain that he had never put human figures in any of his paintings, had never felt any desire to do so. But since the accident, his feelings had changed, and he had a real urge to capture people on canvas.

"Then do it!" Jan encouraged. "Maybe your left hand is a marvelous people-painter, if you'll just give it a chance."

Anton laughed again, delighted with her people-painter expression. "Perhaps you will come and pose for me." He squinted. "I see you on a solitary rock, your golden hair flowing in the breeze, a pensive expression as you wait for a lover to return."

"Waving a hundred-dollar bill in my hand?" The sarcastic comment popped out as Jan eyed Logan's bronzed back.

Anton looked blank. "Pardon?"

"Nothing. Just a bad joke." Jan leaned back in her chair, glad he evidently hadn't made the connection. "Where are you living now?" she asked to change the subject.

"In an apartment belonging to my sister, in Oxnard. I would be pleased to have you come and see my work sometime." He scribbled an address on a scrap of paper. Almost shyly he added, "And I really would like to paint you."

"Hey, you two," Logan called. "I bring you out here to enjoy a sail, and you're so busy talking you don't know whether you're on land or sea."

"But we're enjoying ourselves. At least I am." Anton smiled at Jan. "Would you like something to drink? We brought soft drinks."

"Yes, thank you."

Anton ducked inside the cabin, and immediately Logan swung down beside Jan. "What are you finding so interesting to discuss with Anton?" he asked.

"Oh, this and that. Jealous?" she asked tartly.

"Maybe." He sounded half-serious. "I thought it was me you were so eager to talk to."

"Perhaps it wasn't important after all."

"Actually, I'm glad to see Anton talking to you. He tends to keep too much to himself." Logan spoke with a certain emphasis, as if he wanted to make certain she understood that jealousy had nothing to do with his curiosity. He scowled slightly, obviously still curious about what they were discussing with such absorption, yet reluctant to acknowledge it by asking further questions.

"He's very grateful to you," Jan said. "He says staying at your house helped him through a very difficult time." She kept her voice light, concealing the respect and admiration she felt for all he had done for Anton. She doubted that Logan would want it remarked upon anyway. He was the kind of man who preferred to keep his good deeds as unobtrusive as possible.

"That's what you talked about all this time?" He sounded skeptical.

"Are you worried that we compared notes and perhaps found that you told the story of the Bakersfield trip with a few...ummm...juicy embellishments of a fictional nature?"

"Don't be ridiculous," Logan growled.

Anton stepped out with cans of root beer. Logan accepted one, popping the flip-top lid with a small, savage gesture of frustration. Jan smiled sweetly.

They were headed back toward the harbor entrance now. Jan had been so engrossed in talking to Anton that she hadn't even realized when they changed direction. Logan drained the root beer in a few gulps, squashed the can in one hand, and went back to adjust a rope.

Logan's curiosity had aroused Jan's own curiosity. Why was he so interested in what she and Anton had discussed? A certain uncharacteristic self-consciousness she sensed in Logan further heightened her curiosity. By that time she felt sufficiently at ease with Anton to do a little prying of her own in an effort to find out just what sort of tale Logan had told Anton about her.

She tried several tactics, casually mentioning Bakersfield and her friend's wedding, throwing in a mention of Mrs. Farrington and the art exhibit, and finally bringing up women's lib and how women were much more aggressive these days.

Anton merely looked bewildered by what he obviously considered a haphazard and rather peculiar collection of subjects for conversation. Now it was Jan's turn to be puzzled. Logan had admitted discussing her with Anton. Anton had shown an instant interest in her at that awkward meeting around the hot tub. Just what *had* the two of them discussed about her?

After the sail, the trio had dinner together at a steakhouse. The atmosphere was masculine and the steaks enormous. The men drank foaming mugs of beer, and Jan indulged in a small mountain of onion rings. It was a thoroughly enjoyable, if hardly intimate evening. Anton grew more relaxed and turned out to have a witty sense of humor and a surprising supply of funny anecdotes about everything from once being so engrossed in a sea painting that the tide came in and engulfed him, to, in a desperate moment of financial need years ago, accepting a commission to paint a scene on a bathroom commode lid.

When the evening ended, Logan walked Jan to her car in the steakhouse parking lot. "I haven't heard Anton laugh like that in a long time. He's going to make it. I'm glad you came along today." A warm light in Logan's eyes said more. He glanced reluctantly at Anton waiting in the Ferrari. Since the accident, Anton hadn't driven, and Logan had to drive him back to his sister's apartment in Oxnard. "How soon may I see you again?" The brief words held a rough urgency that sent a heady tingle through Jan.

"I'm pretty well tied up with the show until Thursday."

"Thursday night then." He brushed her lips in a kiss that held a depth of promise in spite of its lightness. In a husky growl, he added, "And don't make any plans to rush home early."

Jan felt as if she was dancing through the week. She had already been looking forward to her Thursday show, and the date with Logan made the day a potent double-header.

This show was different from those Jan had done before, the freedom to experiment another of the advantages of association with a small station. Through mothers she had met on the day-care piece, Jan had rounded up half a dozen adorable little girls. It was to be a pre-Easter show, broadcast live from the studio with Jan and the girls making some unusual little Easter egg dolls and talking about Easter in a warm mother-daughter sort of way. Stephanie's Tuesday guest had been a gourmet cooking expert, and a kitchen set was already in place for them to use.

The night before the show, Jan hard-boiled several dozen eggs and carefully assembled all the other necessary supplies, crayons and egg coloring, bits of felt and ribbon and lace. Thursday morning was hectic. Since the children's mothers were working, Jan had to pick up the little girls at the day-care center, see that they were properly dressed, herd them through numerous bathroom trips, and go over with them what they were going to do on the show. She wanted spontaneity, but not bedlam.

The second hand of the big clock on the studio wall whirled toward the hour, and then a pointing finger signaled to Jan that she was on. She gave the women's news report while a floor assistant kept the girls under control on the kitchen set. During the commercial break, Jan hurried to the set and arranged the girls around her. They looked angelic, their pastel dresses like petals on some sweet wild-flower.

Into the camera, Jan explained to the viewers that today she and the girls were going to demonstrate how to create clever little Easter egg dolls. She made what she hoped was a graceful glide to the refrigerator to get a bowl of the boiled eggs she had stashed there. She swung the door open, careful not to turn her back to the camera. She reached inside for the bowl.

Her fumbling hand found nothing. She said something bright and cheerful to fill in space, but she felt a growing sense of panic. Where *was* the bowl?

Finally she opened the refrigerator door wider and peered inside. She had put five dozen hard-boiled eggs in there not over three hours ago. *Five dozen,* so there would be plenty. They had to be in there somewhere.

But there were *no* eggs. Under the cold glare of the appliance bulb . . . and the hot glare of the camera lights . . . the refrigerator was quite empty.

CHAPTER
Nine

DISASTER. PANIC. WHAT NOW? The whole show was built around those damned eggs! With the ogre eye of the camera on her, impersonally registering every move and expression, Jan's mind spun helplessly. Somehow, with a brightly artificial smile, she managed to ask if someone off-camera would check and see if a few dozen eggs were lying around somewhere. Then she went back to the little girls and tried desperately to make a show out of talking to them. The rough script she had worked out was meaningless without the eggs to create the Easter dolls.

No eggs turned up. The half-hour show stretched out to eternity. Jan felt as if she had spent her entire lifetime under the pitiless glare of the lights, trying frantically to think of something, anything, to say next. With nothing to do, the angelic little girls showed their small-demon sides.

Behind Jan's back, one drew a crayon mustache on another. Two more overturned a chair and wailed at the top of their lungs. Mercifully, someone decided to run part of a file film on birds for the last ten minutes. Jan felt numb.

After the girls were returned to the day-care center, Jan expected—and received—a strong dressing-down from the station manager himself. She accepted the reprimand silently. There was no point in making excuses or accusations, even though there was no doubt in her mind about who was responsible for the disappearance of those all-important eggs. She had caught a glimpse of Stephanie watching from off-camera, standing motionless with a small smile on her face while everyone else scurried around on a futile egg hunt.

Jan was still seething when Logan picked her up that evening. She wasn't a superstitious person normally, but it certainly seemed as if this day were under the control of a vengeful fate that had zeroed in on her. Everything went wrong. At dinner she spilled red wine on her beige wool skirt. An old girlfriend of Logan's, leggy and redheaded and gorgeous, stopped by the table to say hello and give Jan a withering once-over. Jan returned the favor, but it was hard to radiate sophistication and self-confidence with that red blotch on her dress. Jan hadn't intended to tell Logan anything about her on-the-air fiasco today, but to her consternation, he said unexpectedly that he had watched the show on a television set at the office. At any other time, Jan would have found his interest in the show flattering, but now it made her feel defensive and angry.

"I suppose your attitude is the same as Gordon Palmer's. That it was all my fault."

He slanted an eyebrow quizzically, a forkful of steak halted halfway to his mouth. "Wasn't it?"

"Stephanie Trainer deliberately did something with those eggs in order to sabotage my show."

"That's a rather serious charge." Logan sounded guarded. He set the fork down. "Can you prove it?"

"She didn't leave a trail of eggshells, if that's what you

mean," Jan snapped sarcastically. "But I *know*—"

"Stephanie Trainer was also positive that you deliberately leaked the information about her guest's marriage announcement in order to sabotage her show."

"That—that's preposterous!" Jan sputtered. "Surely you don't believe—"

"When two women start battling like a couple of alley cats, I'm not sure whom to believe. I do know that if the infighting keeps up, you're apt to destroy the whole show."

"You're blaming *me?*" Jan gasped in outrage.

"I'm not blaming anyone." Logan's voice had the calm of an ice-covered lake. "I'm just offering my opinion."

"Opinion!" Jan snorted. "When you own the station, I'd say it sounds more like a threat than an opinion."

He shrugged stoically and resumed eating. Jan was suddenly too furious to eat any more, and Logan's calm was doubly infuriating. She hadn't intended to run to him like some tattletale child, but once he knew the facts, the least he could do was to be on her side. The minute he finished eating, she stood up.

"I'm ready to go home now."

"That's exactly where I intend taking you." He snatched up the check, threw a generous tip down on the table, and herded Jan toward the door. Something in the determined set of his mouth made her drag her feet. It hadn't been a foregone conclusion that they would spend the night together, but Jan had more or less assumed it would happen. But not now, not with Logan acting as if she were at least half to blame for the hostilities with Stephanie! He wouldn't dare arrogantly assume—

"I meant *my* home," she said pointedly.

His retort was equally pointed. "So did I."

He drove silently and speedily to the apartment, efficiently hitting on green all the stoplights that usually formed a stop-and-go obstacle course for Jan. Some of her anger had begun to drain off. With conflicting accusations coming at him, Logan could hardly be expected to know who was telling the truth. It was all rather childish anyway, she thought guiltily. Professionals should be able to settle their differences in a professional manner.

At the apartment, he marched her to the door as if it were an assigned duty.

"Would you like to come in for a cup of coffee or a drink . . . or something?" she asked lamely. She wanted to make amends but had too much pride to make an outright apology for something she didn't feel was really her fault. She felt a flush rise to her cheeks as the yard light caught a speculative glint in his eyes. She half-expected him to make some suggestive taunt about her "or something" invitation. He didn't. He was strictly businesslike.

"Thank you, no." No excuses. Just *no*.

"Oh." Jan bit her lower lip. She took a deep breath. "I'm sorry about tonight. I suppose I haven't been very good company. It was just one of those days. If you'd like to come for dinner tomorrow night, perhaps we could get off to a better start."

"Sorry." His tone was brusque. "I'm leaving tomorrow morning. I'll be gone for ten days to two weeks. We're considering buying into some resort property on the Texas Gulf coast, and Aunt Rue and I are going down to investigate the deal."

"Two weeks?" Jan repeated in dismay. Her perspective suddenly shifted, putting today's disaster somewhere in a minor background landscape. Logan was going away for two weeks, and he was leaving with this unpleasant evening splitting a chasm between them. Suddenly she wished that she were a different sort of person, someone bold and charismatic who could say or do something irresistibly seductive. But all that came out was a tentative "Perhaps I'll see you when you get back, then?"

"Perhaps."

"There's an old saying—absence makes the heart grow fonder." She swallowed and blurted out, "I'll miss you."

He looked down at her, his dark eyes enigmatic. "There's another saying—out of sight, out of mind." He leaned over and brushed her lips with a mocking kiss, leaving no doubt as to which course he intended to follow.

Out of sight, out of mind. The words echoed in Jan's

mind all through the long, empty weekend. No doubt they were working for Logan, she thought unhappily. He was down on the Gulf coast wrapped up in his big business deal, probably with a bevy of bikini-clad admirers to soothe his off hours. Jan couldn't say that absence made her heart grow *fonder*. She was precariously aware that, if she acknowledged what she already felt for Logan, she would have to admit it was love. So instead she chafed and fumed and dragged out each and every one of Logan's transgressions for thorough examination, working herself into a self-righteous lather. The one thing she couldn't do, she had to admit sourly, was to put him out of her mind.

On Monday, a small incident gave her something to think about in addition to Logan. She was at the copy machine when she heard voices in the hallway. Stephanie's and Bruce Gurley's.

". . . would make a marvelous inspirational show," Stephanie was saying. "He's an artist and his right hand was mangled in an accident and he's making a comeback by learning to paint with his left hand."

"Sure, sounds like a great idea," Bruce agreed, "but unless you can locate the guy, we can't do anything with it. You aren't even sure of his name, are you?"

"No, but I'm going to talk to a friend who's an art instructor . . ."

The voices faded around the corner as they reached Bruce's office. Jan stood there, momentarily stunned, until she came to her senses and shut off the machine that was spewing copies. They were talking about Anton Bertanoli! And Stephanie was right. Anton's comeback as an artist after his accident would make a terrific inspirational show. A talented person, downed by fate, overcoming obstacles with courage and determination . . . it was a natural. Jan lashed herself mentally for not realizing that earlier. He wasn't female, of course, but his story would surely be an inspiration to women to overcome the obstacles in their own lives. And it was Stephanie's idea, she groaned inwardly. Why hadn't *she* thought of it?

It was late afternoon before Jan's subconscious tossed up a thought that had been churning there all day, a thought that she summarily rejected at first. She dredged it up reluctantly for further examination. An inspirational show with Anton Bertanoli was Stephanie's idea, of course, but Stephanie wasn't even sure of Anton's name, much less how to get in touch with him. The idea might well go no further than that casual hallway conversation.

Of course, what Jan *could* do was go to Stephanie and give her the missing information. Would Stephanie do that if the situation were reversed? Jan asked herself. No way! Stephanie would grab the idea and run with it.

Jan didn't decide to do that, but she did decide to drive over to Oxnard and see Anton and sound him out. After all, he had invited her to come and see his work.

He hadn't given her a telephone number, so she had no way to announce her visit, but his reaction when she appeared at his door that evening was one of pleasure as much as surprise. His apartment served as both a studio and living quarters, and he showed her both finished paintings and work in progress. His newer works were, indeed, a change from the old. The seascapes were warmer, more sunny, somehow softer than his former harshly powerful works. Odd, Jan mused, that his battle with depression would have had that effect. He shyly pointed out his first attempt at painting a portrait, a marvelous study of an old man whose face was etched with lines as timeless as the sea-worn rock behind him. A second painting—just started—was of a little boy discovering some small treasure on a beach. They talked about Anton's work and the possibility of a gallery showing this summer. They casually touched on Logan's absence on the business trip. Finally Jan worked around to the real purpose of her visit.

Anton hesitated, obviously reluctant to do the show, but not wanting to turn her down. He had already mentioned how helpful her talk with him on the sailboat had been; how, when he got discouraged, he reminded himself of all her brother Mike had overcome. Jan pointed out that hearing how Anton had conquered the obstacle of his injured hand could offer similar inspiration to others. By the time she left, he had agreed to do the show.

Jan assured him that she would arrange it so there would be as little inconvenience for him as possible. He needn't come to the station or memorize an involved script. She would bring a videotaping crew to his studio, and he could simply answer her questions naturally. The whole thing wouldn't take more than an afternoon. He gave her a phone number, and she said she'd call as soon as she had everything set up. There was little doubt in her mind that, if Stephanie had asked him to do the show, he would have turned her down flat. The thought served to banish Jan's lingering guilt about her appropriation of Stephanie's idea. Stephanie wouldn't actually have been able to use it anyway.

Jan went to Hank Rossland with the plan the very next day, half-afraid, when she presented it, that Stephanie might already have discussed something similar with him. Evidently she hadn't, however, and he immediately approved Jan's plans and told her to go ahead and work out a schedule with the videotaping crew.

Jan wished that she could ask for secrecy from everyone involved, but she hardly dared do that. It would only arouse curiosity. If there was to be an explosion from Stephanie—and Jan fully expected there would be—she preferred that it come *after* the show was aired, not before, when it could bring everything to a halt in some messy hassle.

Logan telephoned from Texas the night before the scheduled videotaping at Anton's apartment. In his usual way, without preliminaries, he growled, "I miss you, though I'll be damned if I know why, considering how furious you make me sometimes." He sounded resentful, as if his missing her were something for which she was to blame.

Jan was so glad to hear him that not even a trace of peppery retort came to mind. She clung to the phone, wishing it were his warm, muscular hand instead of a cold plastic instrument. "When will you be back?"

"I'm not sure. Aunt Rue is flying home tomorrow, but I'll be here a few days yet. Are you keeping busy?"

Jan momentarily considered telling him about her upcoming show with Anton, but something made her hesitate. Logan had made her promise not to reveal Anton's whereabouts. But she wasn't doing that, of course. Nothing would be mentioned on the show about where he lived or worked. That probably no longer mattered anyway, now that Anton was out on his own and doing so well. A moment later, Jan suddenly realized that it wasn't her professional "keeping busy" to which Logan was referring when he added a more pointed comment.

"I thought perhaps Paul had turned up again and was taking you to places while I was 'out of sight.'"

Jan hesitated before finally saying, "Shelley said he called once while I was out. He wanted me to return his call, but I didn't."

"I see." Was there relief in his voice? She couldn't tell. Maybe he was just curious. But his next words made her think it was more than that. "I'll definitely be home by Saturday. Let's make that sail out to the islands." There was a certain rough possessiveness in his voice.

"I'd like that. I—I'll be looking forward to it."

Jan hung up the phone, feeling a kind of first-date giddiness. Logan sounded as if his out-of-sight, out-of-mind program hadn't been entirely successful after all. The call did something else to Jan, and the admission she had determinedly held back overflowed, like a dam swamped by the floodtide rising behind it. She loved him, loved him, loved him! She felt like doing some idiotically gleeful little jig, and only Shelley's doleful, red-rimmed eyes stopped her. Shelley and her fiancé had just broken up, and Shelley's world was awash in tears.

The videotaping session at Anton's studio went smoothly. He was a little stiff and uncertain at first, but Jan got him absorbed in talking to her before the cameras started rolling. By the time the taping started, he was warm and relaxed. He talked about and showed examples of both his past and present works, freely mentioned his despair and frustration as he tried to switch to his left hand. He brought up the subject of his wife and daughter of his own accord, a subject

Jan had decided to avoid as possibly too sensitive. It definitely added something to the show, however, and Jan found herself surreptitiously wiping a tear from her eyes. By the time the men packed up their equipment, she had no doubts that this would be the best show she had presented. She thanked Anton warmly for his cooperation.

Jan was still exhilarated when Logan called from Ojai Friday evening. Her Bertanoli show would be aired the following Tuesday, ahead of schedule, she had learned today, because Stephanie's scheduled Tuesday guest had canceled. Jan made a polite gesture of saying to Logan that perhaps they should postpone the planned Saturday sail, that he must be tired from his business trip.

She was happy and gratified to hear him say firmly, "Oh, no. We're going sailing. And you'd better be ready on time, or I'll shanghai you right out of the bed or shower or wherever you are."

Jan had a sudden mental image of herself flung naked over Logan's shoulder. An image, she suspected shakily, that wasn't all that improbable, given Logan's determination when he made up his mind to do something!

She was ready at the early hour he named, however, half-regretting that she wasn't daring enough to see if he'd carry out his threat. She had packed a lunch, including a bottle of wine. She wore white jeans and a shapeless blue sweatshirt that didn't look shapeless at all once she slipped it on. Her hair was plaited into one long golden braid hanging down her back, with a flowered scarf to control the independent tendrils that escaped. Lunch and jacket in hand, Jan met Logan at the door when he rang the bell.

His hands caught her by the shoulders. "You look all of fourteen years old," he announced. "How the hell come I missed you so much?" he added huskily.

"Maybe you're a secret pedo- whatever that word is that means a man with an abnormal interest in little girls," she suggested tartly.

His gaze slid to the rounded mounds of her breasts, and his hands journeyed leisurely to the curve of her waist, then crept beneath the sweatshirt to contact bare skin. The touch was electric, as if something within her leaped out to meet him. "I think my interests are pretty normal," he said meaningfully. Lazily, as one hand slid around to explore her breast and found the tip straining and rigid, he added, "So are yours."

"I know that if we don't get this sail under way pretty soon, we're going to wind up . . . somewhere else."

"You're right." He laughed but not without an undertone of regret. "And I suppose your roommate is home." He leaned over and kissed her, and Jan felt that same leaping, electric reaction. Too soon he broke off the kiss, leaving her not dissatisfied, but breathlessly wanting more. He grinned nonchalantly, but Jan knew that he wasn't unaffected. In close contact, male arousal was hardly unnoticeable.

At the marina Logan wasted no time getting the sail under way. The day was sunny but brisk. The islands looked hazy-blue in the distance. Logan said it was a good thing they had planned the sail for today. A storm was supposed to move in late that night or early the next day. The water wasn't really rough, but it seemed a bit boisterous, as if it enjoyed giving the small boat an unexpected toss now and then.

The sail out to the islands took several hours, longer than Jan had expected. The islands, little more than blue silhouettes from shore, took on shape and character as the sailboat drew closer. They were higher and rougher than Jan had realized. Rocky, primeval-looking cliffs rose abruptly out of the sea. A misting of fog mingled with the spray of waves climbing in endless assault against the stark cliffs. The island they were approaching, Logan said, was Anacapa. Far off to the south was Santa Barbara Island. Stretching in a westerly direction from Anacapa were the other islands that made up Channel Islands National Park. The two largest, Santa Cruz and Santa Rosa, though a part of the park, were actually privately owned. San Miguel Island, the most westerly island, was a major elephant-seal rookery. In order to land there, a special permit was needed. Seals and sea lions were common around all the islands.

A sleek brown head with bewhiskered face examined the sailboat with what seemed a curiosity equal to Jan's own. Then, with an impudent flip of his body, the sea lion disappeared beneath a breaking wave. He was only the first of many that cavorted around them.

At the eastern tip of Anacapa was Arch Rock, a rough natural archway carved by eons of the persistent sea. Flocks of gulls and other sea birds swooped and jostled for prize positions atop the arch. Below, the water was a tangled mass of kelp. The long strands moved in the clear water with a languid, almost seductive motion. The sound of sea lions barking formed a strange chorus from the rocks.

"It's marvelous . . . fantastic!" Jan breathed.

"We'll sail around for a while, eat our lunch on board, and then hike the trails on Anacapa."

They saw an endless array of jagged, timeless cliffs; brown pelicans, with their strange combination of clumsiness and grace; vaulted caves; and more seals and sea lions, including some of the elephant seals, which were named for their peculiar facial shape. Water slapped gently on the sides of the boat, crashed on the rocky shores, and shot skyward at an impressive blowhole. Jan ate her lunch standing in the cockpit because she didn't want to miss seeing a thing.

When they went ashore to hike, Jan was surprised to find that the rolling plateau above the cliffs wasn't quite as barren as she had expected. At this time of year small, delicate wildflowers were blooming, and here and there was the flamboyant yellow flash of a flowery shrub that resembled a giant sunflower. Logan called it coreopsis. The mist gradually thickened as they hiked, and droplets collected on Jan's thick pigtail and jeweled her eyelashes. The Coast Guard's automatic foghorn came on and boomed its rhythmic warning signal. Jan loved the damp sea scent, the melancholy sound of the foghorn, the swirling mist . . . and Logan's hand holding hers tightly. They hadn't talked of themselves this day, merely enjoyed the glorious beauties of nature, their conversation limited to an exclamation of something new and fascinating to see. But something about Logan's possessive grip said more than words.

"Hey, I think we'd better get back to the boat. That wind is really starting to blow!" Logan exclaimed as a gust whipped Jan's braid like a golden flag.

At that moment they were at the farthermost point on the trail, a jutting promontory overlooking a rugged expanse of cliff that angled roughly down to a sea that had turned menacingly tempestuous. Before they were halfway back to the boat, they were fighting the wind just to stay upright. The mist changed to a pelting rain that stung Jan's face.

"I think the weatherman was wrong!" The wind whipped Logan's voice away, making the words sound distant even though he was right next to her, his arm encircling her shoulders protectively. "That storm is here now!" An ominous rumble of thunder emphasized his words.

The wind...the rain...the otherwordly sound of the foghorn...rumbles of thunder...the strange, surrealistic barking of the now-unseen sea lions...they all combined in a scene that was both frightening and exhilarating as Jan and Logan fought their way to the boat. Like a sneak thief, the spring storm had crept in under cover of the mists and engulfed them.

On the boat, Logan pushed Jan into the protective shelter of the cabin, but not before she was drenched. He braved wind and rain to move the boat under engine power to a more protected portion of the cove. By the time he dropped anchor and ducked inside, he was soaked to the skin, his hair a wet, unruly mane.

Jan handed him a towel and he wiped his face, only to have rivulets trickle off his hair and wet it again. He exuded a warm, wet male-animal vitality that promptly steamed over the small window of the cabin.

"You look like a Viking," Jan announced. With a critical tilt of her head she added impishly, "On a day that the pillaging didn't go too well."

"I believe the usual term for the Vikings' activities is 'pillaging and raping,'" Logan retorted. His blue eyes gleamed behind tawny wet lashes. "And since I haven't gotten around to the second part yet..."

Jan laughed, but she felt a certain breathlessness. "Well,

I don't think there's time for that. If we're going to get back to the marina before—"

"Before what? Have you looked outside lately?"

Jan rubbed moisture from the window and peered out. No trace of the California shoreline remained beyond the sheets of falling rain. Barely visible outside the shelter of the cove were rolling waves tossing spumes of white froth. Jan turned back to Logan, her dark eyes wide.

"You mean—"

"Dry my back."

While she was looking out the window, he had stripped off his wet shirt. He tossed the towel to her. Using both hands, she rubbed the towel over his damp skin. He rounded his shoulders forward to make a smooth, taut curve of his back. His bronzed skin was deceptively smooth, and she could feel the strength of the hard muscles playing beneath it. Without meaning to, her thumbs traced the rippled line of his spine, sending a small tremor of reaction shooting along her own spine.

He turned around. "Okay. Now you."

"I'm not wet!"

"No?" He squeezed the sleeve of her sweatshirt between thumb and forefinger until several drops plopped to the floor. "I'll get a dry towel."

Reluctantly Jan turned and slipped the wet sweatshirt over her head. Before she could organize a protest, Logan had efficiently unsnapped her bra. Only her hands held the honey-colored lace over her breasts. With the same efficiency, he pried her crossed hands loose and the bra tumbled to the edge of the bed.

"This is no time to be modest," he stated calmly.

With long, methodical strokes he dried her back thoroughly, squeezing the golden braid with a firm grip. Finally he turned her to face him. She could feel rivulets trickling across her breasts. He watched in fascination as a drop slid across the skin and then clung to one pink tip. The drop hung there like an exotic jewel, poised and glistening. With sudden impatience, Logan dipped his head and captured the clinging drop with his mouth . . . and then enveloped the sweet fullness of the breast to which the drop clung. A sound rumbled through him, a husky mixture of pleasure and desire. Jan's fingers moved through his still-damp hair, holding his head to her and pressing her cheek against the crisp roughness of his hair.

He moved to the other breast, leaving the first one taut and damp from the sweet caress of his mouth. "Do you know," he murmured between the delicate swirls and tugs on her breast, "that all the time I was working on that damned Texas resort deal, I was thinking about you? I probably let them get away with the deal of the century."

"I—I doubt that."

He straightened up, running his hands down to her waist and almost encircling it with his broad grip. His legs spread and braced against the rocking of the boat, he pulled her to him. Her breasts nestled in the soft tangle of golden hair on his chest, and the sinewy cords of his thighs tightened against her. He had the primitive scent of sea-dampened skin and hair, and a subtle but even more intoxicating aura of raw male virility. His hands moved down to cup the damp curve of her jeans and lift her against him. There was no mistaking the vital throb of his masculinity.

"We're going to get chilled and catch pneumonia if we don't get out of these wet clothes," he whispered.

"I'm not . . . chilled." A warmth was coming from within her. She could feel it radiating outward through her skin, like an inner sunshine. Her hands were around his neck, toying with that familiar curl about which she felt a sudden almost fierce possessiveness. "But if *you* are afraid of wet clothes and pneumonia . . ."

With an unplanned recklessness, she stepped backward and fumbled with the metal button at the waistband of his jeans. He looked startled momentarily, then grinned and folded his arms across his chest. She struggled futilely with button and zipper and stiff wet denim that clung tenaciously around his lean hips.

Finally he reached down and pulled her into his arms again. His blue eyes gleamed with a mixture of amusement and male desire. "This is all very nice, and I can't say I'm not enjoying it," he murmured huskily. "But sometimes speed is more important than technique."

"To prevent—pneumonia?" she inquired.

He grinned wickedly. "Not necessarily."

He stripped out of the stubborn wet jeans in moments, and his deft hands swiftly conquered the clinging resistance of her own wet clothing. He swept her up in his arms, deposited her in the cavelike alcove of the bed, and stretched out beside her.

"Are we really stranded here for the night?" Jan asked.

His fingertips traced a featherly line around the sensitive inner curve of her hipbone. "We may be stranded here forever, now that I have you in my arms." Her legs were captured under the long, lean line of one of his flung over them. The roving hand moved up to caress the corner of her lips with a thumb, and his mouth hovered only inches away. "My sweet, sweet January. Not nearly so cold and aloof as her name implies." He laughed softly. "But I think she lacks experience in the art of undressing a man. Something to which we will have to devote much time and practice . . ."

"You're laughing at me," Jan accused suspiciously. She raised up, halfway intending to scoot out of bed, but his hands caught and lifted her in the air over him as he rolled over on his back. Her breasts hung over him like some exotic ripe fruit, and he feasted on them as if they were delicious beyond belief, moving from one to the other with leisurely equality.

Jan floated, her mind and senses spinning dreamily with the exquisite sensations drifting through her. She felt like one of those languid, seductively waving strands of kelp, boneless, the control of her body located somewhere outside herself. She gave herself up to the drifting, floating feeling, spinning lazily on a tropical sea of exquisite pleasure. Logan lifted her higher, trailing a line of kisses to her navel, then returning to the delicious ripeness of her breasts.

She became aware of a heaviness centered somewhere in her lower body, a heaviness that clung to Logan like some powerful magnetic force pulling that part of their bodies ever more closely together. And then it was no longer an unfocused heaviness but a throbbing, demanding force within her, an ache of emptiness.

With a rumbled growl deep in his throat, Logan reversed their positions, and then the emptiness was no more. The tropical sea within her turned tempestuous, and then it was a raging storm between them. Jan lost all consciousness of the storm outside, of the irregular toss of the windblown waves. She was only aware of a complete and perfect union, a joining so total that their bodies moved together as a single pulsebeat. The rhythm moved stronger and higher, climbing like a musical note, until the music and pulse blended together in a cosmic song of ecstasy that coursed through her and through him and through them together, until there was no *him* or *her* . . . just the incredible oneness.

Neither of them moved for a long time. Jan had no idea how long it was before she became aware of a sense of the separate existence of her own body, her own being. Logan stirred, as if he, too, had just become aware, regretfully, that they existed separately, and perhaps his weight was heavy on her. He rolled to one side.

"Was I too rough?" he asked contritely. "I didn't mean to be quite so impatient."

Rough? No. Impatient? Perhaps. Perfect? Yes, oh yes! She ran her outspread fingers through the soft curl of chest hair, ruffling it as she might the fur of a purring cat. "I'm not going to make any comments, or you'll just get conceited."

He laughed softly, secure in the knowledge of her complete and utter satisfaction.

"Do you suppose this is how a waterbed feels?" Jan asked dreamily. The motion of the rocking boat was more rhythmic now, less tempestuously tossed. Or was it that the tempest was gone from within her now, replaced by a serene tranquillity?

"I'm sure I don't know. We'll have to try one sometime. We'll have to try lots of things. And then we'll try them all again."

His voice held husky laughter, but there was a certain

wistfulness in hers when she countered, "Will we?"

He raised up on one elbow and looked down at her. Her chaste braid had come undone, and her hair spread in a rippled golden fan across the pillow.

"Are you still worrying that I told Anton some titillating tale about a female wildcat who hired me for a date and then made passionate love with me on my sailboat?"

"From the extent of his rather curious appraisal of me, you must have told him something rather 'titillating,'" Jan retorted. Her words held a certain tart sharpness, but there was a languid softness in her body that made withdrawal from his embrace impossible.

"Perhaps that depends on what you consider titillating," Logan mused. "What I told him was that I had met the most beautiful girl in the world and I thought I was falling in love with her. Since that wasn't the kind of thing I told Anton often . . . or ever," he corrected, after a moment's thoughtful reflection, "I'm sure his curiosity *was* aroused."

"Oh!" The small explosion was more expelled breath than word. "And—and how do you feel now?" Her breath held unconsciously, tightened in her chest until it became almost an ache while his eyes studied her in the near darkness.

"I think," he said softly, "that I was quite correct in my initial assessment of the situation."

"You sound like a businessman discussing a—a Texas resort deal!" Jan objected indignantly.

"I intend to make loving you the most important business of all." He kissed her on the tip of the nose. "But first we need some revitalization in the form of *food*."

They made a meal of lunch leftovers, canned chili heated on the small stove, and slightly damp crackers, all washed down with the bottle of wine that hadn't been opened at lunch. Because everything else was still wet, Jan dined in her panties and bra, Logan in his briefs, and they giggled like a couple of children playing hooky from school.

Afterward, grimacing at the feel of wet denim, Logan slid into his clothes and went outside to make sure everything was secure for the night. When he came inside, Jan, making a pretense that it was a bothersome duty, dried him off again, rubbing and patting solicitously until it became apparent that she was returning more often than was really necessary to certain portions of his anatomy.

In mock anger, threatening dire punishments for her audacity, Logan tossed her down on the bed and proceeded to "punish" her so deliciously that she felt a spinning delirium.

Finally they slept, their bodies fitted together like spoons, his hand gently cupping her breast. Jan was vaguely aware of him moving around several times in the night as he kept a protectively watchful eye on their situation, but she slept feeling warm and secure. The sound of the foghorn, reassuringly regular, was a comforting background noise. She probably would have wakened if it had unexpectedly stopped.

By morning the cove was as serene as a lake, sunlight dancing on the gentle swells beyond the cove. They spread their still-damp jeans in the sunshine. Logan dug out an old pair of swim trunks to wear, but Jan scampered around in a sweatshirt and panties. They breakfasted on what was available—canned vegetable soup and coffee—and explored the island shorelines further.

"Some sailor you are, getting us marooned out here for the night," Jan teased once, her hands on her hips as she eyed the California shoreline glistening fresh-washed in the sunshine. "Or was this something you had all planned ahead of time?"

"My dear January," he said loftily, "I may be able to move corporations, perhaps even dislodge a minor mountain or two, but I have absolutely no control over the weather." He grinned. "However, I'm not above taking advantage of whatever the fates may send."

Jan cocked her head, suddenly seeing something in him she hadn't noticed before. His grin wasn't absolutely perfect. It was just slightly lopsided, a small imperfection usually lost in the dazzling sight of his ruggedly handsome features. It was an endearing smile, and Jan's throat suddenly felt oddly choked.

"I love you," she said softly. Her words were lost in a sudden outburst of yelping from sea lions squabbling nearby, but it didn't really matter.

Finally, regretful that the idyll must come to an end, they headed back to the Ventura harbor. But it wasn't an end, Jan knew with a joyous singing in her heart. It was really a beginning. Whenever she looked at Logan his eyes were on her, laughing and tender and loving. Before they parted, they made a dinner date for Wednesday night, the first night Logan had free of business engagements.

The world was still glorious when Jan's videotaped show with Anton Bertanoli aired at midday Tuesday. Linda came running in to say, "It was terrific. I cried!" And she had the tear-glistened eyes to prove it. Mr. Palmer, never one to be overly generous with praise, gave her a gruffly approving comment in the hallway. Several calls came in from viewers. Hank Rossland said he was going to rerun a few minutes of the tape on the local evening news. Stephanie was away from the station for the day, so there was a potential explosion yet to come there, but Jan felt on top of the world, ready for anything.

But there was one thing for which she was totally unprepared.

She was fixing a sandwich for dinner that evening, eating alone because Shelley had gone out for a discussion with her ex-fiancé. The doorbell rang, and even before Jan could reach the door, the bell buzzed again in a series of impatient, staccato bursts.

"Logan!" Jan exclaimed, startled, as she opened the door partway. Had she made a mistake? Were they supposed to have dinner tonight instead of—

Her thoughts broke off abruptly as she realized this was no pleasant social call. A white outline of fury was etched around Logan's compressed mouth. His hands hung clenched into fists at his sides, and his shoulders had a ready-to-lunge look. With a crash of his fist, he shoved the door open.

CHAPTER
Ten

LOGAN STRODE INSIDE, and Jan scrambled out of his way. She had the distinct impression that he would have walked right over her if she hadn't moved.

"Logan, what's wrong?" But even as she gasped the words, she suspected what had happened. He'd seen or heard about the show with Anton Bertanoli and disapproved. She felt a moment of doubt as she backed away from the stalking advance of his formidable figure. The door thundered behind him as he slammed it with a vicious shove. Then she came to a defiant halt, her head jerked up. It was a *good* show, wonderfully inspirational, and he had no right to be so livid with fury! "I suppose you're unhappy about—"

"Have you any idea where Anton is?" he cut in roughly.

"Anton?" Jan repeated in surprise at the unexpected question. "No, of course not." She eyed his clenched fists warily, uneasily aware that only supreme self-control kept them at his sides. He was wearing a dark, well-cut business suit, but his tie was off and the collar unbuttoned. There was an inexplicable aura of danger about his careless appearance, as if at any moment he might completely discard the trappings of civilized behavior.

"He's disappeared. I can't find him anywhere. I had a call at the office from him this afternoon, right after that show of yours was on." He spat out the words about her show as if they were poison in his mouth. "He was so upset, he was hardly coherent. I've been looking for him ever since."

"But . . . but I don't understand. He seemed fine at the taping. Everyone thought the show was marvelous!"

"Oh, yes, it was 'marvelous,'" Logan mimicked cruelly. "Very effective. Especially that little tear you managed to let slide down your cheek. I'm sure everyone is praising you to high heaven. And that's all you care about, isn't it? You never cared a damn about the effect the show might have on Anton!"

A leaden ball lumped in Jan's stomach. She retreated under the onslaught of Logan's fury and scorn. She put the barrier of a chair between them, and her hands clutched the wooden back with stiff fingers. "What—what do you mean?" She felt an awful premonition of doom.

"Anton had improved greatly in the last few weeks. He was coming along fine, both emotionally and physically. And then you put the cold, impersonal eye of the camera on his work, first the work he'd done before the accident, then on painting he's done more recently. It wiped him out. You made him see—at least in his own eyes—that his new work is no match for his old. He feels he has utterly failed. It was too much for him."

"But that isn't true!" Jan gasped. "I like his new work better. It shows more warmth and understanding and compassion."

"Qualities in which you are notably lacking." Logan spat out the words with a mouth twisted in disgust.

Jan swayed under the assault of waves of fury and disdain vibrating from him. "But I had no idea..." she protested faintly. "I'd never deliberately do anything to hurt him. And I was careful not to say exactly where he was living because I'd promised—"

"You never gave *him* a minute's thought. You were thinking only about yourself. Your glory. But it was too soon for him!" For a moment Logan seemed almost to forget his fury at her in his agonized groan of concern for his troubled friend. "Couldn't you see that? His self-esteem is still too shaky, his emotional condition too delicately balanced. Yes, someday, when he was emotionally ready to step back into the public spotlight, a show like that might have been good for him. But it was too soon."

"But where would he go? What would he do?" Jan spread her hands in bewildered appeal as she moved out from behind the protection of the chair. Suddenly the possibility of what Anton might do became horribly, sickeningly clear to her. "He wouldn't—" Her tongue felt thick. She couldn't say the word.

Logan could. "Suicide? Yes, I'm afraid so." His lips slid back to reveal even, white teeth in a savage parody of a smile. "Are you afraid his untimely suicide might reflect unfavorably on your show?"

"Logan...please..." Jan returned to clutch the chair until her fingers ached.

"What the hell ever made you decide to do such a show anyway?"

Jan's mind gyrated like some wildly out-of-control space capsule. Was it true? Had she done something to plunge Anton back into his bottomless hole of despair and depression...and beyond? The leaden ball churned in rising nausea within her. "No..." She shook her head in helpless denial, her protest aimed as much at her own burgeoning guilt as at Logan. "It was Stephanie's idea..."

Jan hardly realized she had spoken aloud until Logan's expression changed. The fury was no less, but something was added to it now, the ruthlessness of an inquisitor determined to get at the truth. Yet, when he spoke, his voice was soft. Dangerously soft, like quicksand waiting to trap her.

"I didn't see any evidence of Stephanie on the show."

Jan swallowed convulsively, painfully regretting that blurt about Stephanie. The blame was hers, not Stephanie's. She was the one who had talked Anton into doing the show. "It was Stephanie's idea to begin with, but she didn't know enough about the situation to do anything with it, so I—" She broke off, aware of yet another change in the expressions rampaging across Logan's face.

"You stole Stephanie's idea." It was a glacial statement, not a question.

"No! I mean, it—it was hardly even in the idea stage!" Jan floundered, writhing under the impalement of his deadly gaze. "Stephanie didn't even know his name."

"But you knew his name. You knew all about him, his past problems, where to reach him, how to play on his emotions to persuade him to do what you wanted." Logan's chest expanded in a deep breath before he let it out with another explosive accusation. "I thought I could trust you, but I was wrong. You're conniving and opportunistic. You took advantage of a friendship you'd made through me to further your own greedy ambitions. You used *me*."

Jan's mouth moved in automatic denial, but no sound came out. All she could do was shake her head helplessly. Because it was true...true! She had used confidential information she had received through her relationship with Logan.

"You know what Stephanie did to me!" she cried. But even as she said the words, she regretted them.

"I'm not interested in your feuds with Stephanie," he gritted. "What I care about is what you've done to a good, decent guy who was trying his damndest to make it. Jan, up until this moment, I don't think I've really known you at all. I saw you as a hardworking, ambitious woman, but at the same time warm and sweet and vulnerable...and caring." He sounded more weary than angry now. "I had some momentary doubts when you lied on the application form. But I was willing to overlook that, because I knew the reasons behind it. I didn't think it was important—probably more an unfortunate impulse than a real attempt to deceive. But perhaps I should have realized that it signified something more about your character. Maybe something I didn't *want* to see, because I was falling in love with you."

He walked over to the window and stood with his back to her. He looked immovable, as uncompromising as a mountain blotting out the fading evening light. Jan slumped to the sofa. He turned back to her, his face an inscrutable mask now with cruel, glittering eyes that bored into her soul as he went on in a deadly calm voice.

"I thought that polished, glossy exterior you present to the world was just a protective shell. But I was wrong. That hard exterior goes all the way through. The woman I fell in love with was warm and wonderful and open. She could laugh at herself and care about someone else. She made me feel... protective. But that woman isn't you. She doesn't exist. Because the real you is hard and grasping and uncaring. And devious and unscrupulous."

The cruelly blunt words hit Jan with dull, thudding blows. Was there no end to them, no end to the depths of the scorn he felt for her?

She tried to gather the scraps of her pride. "If you're finished—"

"No, I am not finished." He smiled grimly. "Let me briefly—ah—recapitulate exactly what you did. You stole another person's idea. You used confidential information obtained through your relationship with me to make use of the idea. And you put the idea into action without a single thought about its effect on the central figure involved." He ticked off the items as coldly as if this were an impersonal court of law and he the prosecuting attorney. And judge. And executioner. "I'm sure Paul would be proud of you. You used his type of tactics exactly."

Jan's slumped head and downcast eyes flew up. "Paul!" she echoed meaninglessly.

"I was wrong about you and Paul. You're two of a kind. You fully deserve each other. I suggest that you waste no more time before returning his phone call."

Logan turned and strode to the door. A chair in his pathway crashed to the floor, but he paid no more heed to it than to Jan huddled stunned on the sofa. He wrenched the door open and Jan steeled herself for a shuddering slam, but none came. The door closed almost softly, with a small, deadly click. The sound of eternity closing, shutting her away from Logan forever and ever.

She sat there motionless and numb while the spring dusk deepened gently to darkness around her. The phone rang once. She merely looked at it. Eventually it stopped ringing. She didn't notice when.

In spite of Logan's bitterly scathing words that spared her nothing in their cruelty, Jan could feel no anger with him. She was too overwhelmed with remorse and guilt for what she had done. She, of all people, after having lived with her brother's depression and despair, should have known what a fragile, delicately balanced thing Anton's emotional state was. There was no way she could have known the particular impact the show might have on him, but she should have realized that something disastrous could happen. And she hadn't. She had just blundered ahead.

Two of a kind. You and Paul are two of a kind.

Logan's words echoed inside her head, reverberating down an endless hallway until her temples thundered with them. She shook her head in wild protest. No, that wasn't true! She and Paul were worlds apart. She had rejected him. That was proof, wasn't it? And then Logan's accusing words were replaced by other words. Paul's coldly practical words. *An idea belongs to the person who knows how to use it.*

Yes, she had rejected Paul, but she hadn't rejected his philosophy or standards or methods. She had *used* them. Lied on the application, just as he had suggested. Stolen Stephanie's idea. Used it without a thought for the consequences to anyone but herself. Jan felt an almost over-powering sense of self-loathing.

How could she have done it? How *could* she? Was she really all the despicable things Logan accused her of being? Were her eyes so glued to her own selfish goals that she couldn't see anything else? Adele had advised her to reach for the rainbow of success, and like a child stretching for bright colors overhead, she had reached. She had touched the shimmering edges of the rainbow. She had her poignant TV show, her compliments, her victory over Stephanie. But up close the colors of the rainbow weren't so radiantly glowing. The rainbow was ragged around the edges, tarnished with ruthless ambition and greed. Or was it, she wondered bitterly, just her own tainted touch that had tarnished the rainbow?

Logan was gone forever, driven away by what she had done. The magic of their lovemaking, the tender, loving light in his eyes, the laughter and teasing... all gone, gone. The thought was a powerful force swirling her into a bottomless void. She was a small, falling figure calling endlessly in helpless despair, "But I love you. I love you, I love you..."

She must have slept. She became aware of a painful crick in her neck and a numb arm beneath her body twisted awkwardly on the sofa. She moved to the bed but couldn't summon the will to remove her crumpled clothes.

She woke again at first light of dawn, a bad taste in her mouth and a raw, scratchy feeling in her eyes. The emptiness in her stomach wasn't so much hunger as a vague awareness that she hadn't eaten the night before. She stumbled to the bathroom, slapped cold water on her face, and scrubbed her teeth savagely. Shelley's bed hadn't been slept in. Maybe she and her fiancé had patched up their differences.

With a strange, detached feeling of watching herself, Jan changed clothes, fixed coffee, toast, and eggs, and forced the food down. She would need the strength to enable her to do what she must do today. Logan was gone, lost to her forever. The knowledge sent her spinning toward that same bottomless void into which she had swirled helplessly the night before. Strange still-life images of Logan clicked through her mind—Logan flashing her a pirate grin from beside a billowing sail... Logan's face in closeup, his eyes half-closed, a sheen of passion-induced perspiration on his tanned forehead... Logan naked, pagan in the moonlight...

There was a yesterday feeling about the images, as if they clicked off the passing of her carefree youth.

With grim resolution, drawing on some inner reservoir of strength, Jan switched off the images and held herself suspended above the whirlpool force that sucked her toward the void. Later the yawning void might draw her into its darkest depths, but first she must do whatever she could to right the wrong she had done to Anton. If it wasn't already too late.

Where would he go in his despair? Logan knew Anton so much better than she did, and he hadn't been able to find Anton. She searched her mind methodically, dredging up bits and pieces of the conversations she had had with him. Only three conversations to go on, she thought, fighting a feeling of helplessness. The day on the sailboat, the evening in his studio, the afternoon of the videotaping.

She drove first to Anton's apartment-studio in Oxnard. There was always the remote possibility that he had returned there. He hadn't. A note from Logan, asking Anton to get in touch with him, fluttered from the mailbox. The main house was empty also. Jan recalled Anton mentioning that his sister was visiting relatives back east.

He must be somewhere along the coast then. He had always been drawn to the sea. But where? The miles of scenic coastline suddenly seemed endless. Would he seek out some secluded rocky point he had once painted? Try to walk out his despair on some lonely beach? The search seemed terrifyingly impossible, yet she set out to find him. She drove as far down the coast as Malibu and worked her way methodically up the coast. The task would have been easier if he'd been driving and she could search for a particular car, but he hadn't resumed driving yet. Why, oh why hadn't that given her a clue that his emotional balance was still dangerously shaky? she wondered in a despairing moment of self-chastisement.

Once she spotted a lonely figure poised on an outcropping of rock above a thundering surf. She scrambled frantically over a raw jumble of rocks to reach him, frightened by the way he was staring into the surf. But the figure wasn't

Anton, and the poised stance she thought was a readiness to jump was merely an interest in a packing crate disintegrating on the rocks below. Another time she slowed her car beside a stocky, dark-haired figure trudging along the shoulder of the highway, sure she had found Anton, only to have an unfamiliar face glance up at her with a too-friendly leer.

She kept the car radio playing, half-expecting to hear at any moment some brief, impersonal account of a suicide. Vaguely she realized she had never contacted the television station about her absence today. It didn't seem important, not even when she recalled that a crucial budget conference was scheduled for today. Let Stephanie control the meeting. It didn't matter.

Her afternoon search ranged north of Ventura. Once she thought she spotted the secluded crescent of beach where she and Logan had built a fire and picknicked. The cove was empty now, but her mind's eye superimposed two figures on the sand, two figures playing at love, teasing each other with wine and kisses. The taste of both lingered like a sweet pain in her mouth. Later she thought she actually saw Logan driving out of a beach parking lot. Was he searching too? Or was she only imagining him? That was all she had of him now—imagination and memories.

Darkness forced Jan to abandon her beach search, but still she didn't give up. She returned to Anton's apartment, but Logan's note still fluttered forlornly from the mailbox. The wind had torn the scrap of paper, and Jan carefully made it secure again. The apartment had a strangely abandoned, long-empty feel.

Jan returned to her car, fighting an overwhelming feeling of defeat. Where would Anton go tonight, alone and despairing? He could still be on the beach. There were dozens—hundreds!—of places she could have missed him. Yet she had the oddly positive feeling that it wasn't the ocean he loved to which he had gone after all. What else had he loved? His wife and child.

The fire in which they perished had happened here in Ventura, that much Jan knew. Were Anton's wife and child buried here? She felt a tingle of hope. Yes, he might go to their graves! The small hope sank again. It was after hours and all the official local agencies where she might ask questions were closed. Surely the cemeteries, too, were closed at this late hour.

And then where would a man go? To drown himself in drink? Suddenly Jan realized that wasn't a farfetched possibility. Anton had confessed ruefully that, after his wife's death, he'd been for a short time well on his way to developing a drinking problem. What was it he had said? "I spent all my evenings and half my days sitting on a bar stool at the—"

The name hung tantalizingly just out of reach on the edges of Jan's memory. What name had he given? The Whale's Head? The Dolphin Bar. No . . . but it was something like that, something to do with an animal or bird. The Pelican's Perch! Yes, that was it.

Jan found a telephone booth and frantically thumbed the ragged phone book, looking for The Pelican's Perch. Yes, there it was! She instantly memorized the address, stopped at a gas station, and groaned as a bored attendant shrugged, "I dunno," to her request for directions. An attendant at another gas station was more helpful, and finally she was pulling into the parking lot beside a neon-lit tavern.

It was a seedy-looking place. A blue haze of smoke hung in the air as Jan stepped hesitantly inside. Surely Anton wouldn't be *here,* she thought in dismay as her gaze roamed tables cluttered with beer mugs and surrounded by faces that seemed terrifyingly anonymous. She couldn't just wander among them, peering into faces. Taking a deep breath, she approached a bartender drying glasses behind the counter.

"I'm looking for someone. Dark complexion and hair, stocky build, late thirties. He's an artist, but he—he probably seems very depressed. I think he used to come in here a lot."

The bartender's eyes roamed the counter and then he jerked a thumb toward a figure hunched over a drink at the far end. "Him?"

Jan had to look twice. The heavy haze of smoke burned her eyes. Yes, it was Anton. She hesitated, uncertain what to do now that she had found him. "Is he drunk?"

"Nah. He's been nursing a coupla drinks all evening. Maybe better off if he'd get drunk and forget whatever it is that's eating on him."

Hesitantly Jan approached the slumped figure wearing a rumpled white shirt. "Hello, Anton."

He looked up, and pain wrenched Jan's heart at the unexpected way his face lit up. He could look at her like that after what she had done to him! "Jan!" Then, as if he had just remembered something, the glow died. "Buy you a drink?" His voice held no anger, only defeat.

"No, I don't think so. Let me take you back to your apartment."

He made no response, and as soon as she said the words she knew they were wrong anyway. Taking him back to a lonely apartment to brood would do no good.

"May I talk to you?"

His body twitched in a motion that Jan took signified acceptance, and she tried to convey how she felt about his new work, how much everyone cared about him. She mentioned her brother Mike again.

Anton's only response was a despondent, "Mike succeeded. I failed."

Jan felt a mounting desperation. Anton was more than she could handle alone, and there was only one person she could turn to for help. No! She couldn't call Logan, not after the things he had said to her!

"We're closing in ten minutes, miss," the bartender said, not unkindly. "Better take your friend home."

What time was it? Bleary-eyed, Jan held up her wrist to get a better look at her watch. Almost 2:00 A.M. Reluctantly she asked the bartender about a phone and then dialed Logan's number. He answered on the third ring, instant wakefulness in his voice. In concise terms, Jan explained the situation. He offered to come. Jan said the bar was closing, so she would bring Anton to Logan's house.

Anton was apathetic and offered no resistance when Jan told him where they were going. She wrapped a seat belt around him and locked the door on his side of the car before slipping into the driver's seat. He seemed asleep when the car pulled up in front of Logan's brightly lit house.

Wearing jeans and an unbuttoned shirt with the shirttails hanging around his lean hips, Logan stood waiting under the arched entryway. He had evidently watched for the approaching headlights. Anton walked into the house under his own power, lightly guided by Logan's supporting hand. Jan went as far as the door with them.

"I'll put him upstairs for tonight and get him to his doctor tomorrow," Logan said.

"Yes. Good." Jan was so tired her mind felt blurry, as if the blue haze of the tavern had infiltrated her brain. Wearily she turned to go back to her car. Her task was finished.

"You'd better have a cup of coffee. You look as if you need it. There's a pot on the breakfast bar. Second door—"

Jan shook her head. "No, thanks. I just want to get home."

"You need the coffee. And I want to talk to you."

Jan looked at him, blinking and shaking her head to clear a momentary double-vision. She was so tired, so bone-deep tired. Logan was holding an unresisting Anton lightly by one elbow. There was a commanding power and strength about him that was beyond her will to resist. It was easier to acquiesce than argue. She'd have a cup of coffee to brace her for the drive back to Ventura, then slip out before Logan returned from getting Anton settled upstairs.

She found the breakfast bar and poured a cup of steaming black coffee, then promptly scalded her mouth, which—if nothing else—at last served to jolt her wide awake and sharpen her nerves. She couldn't linger here. Logan would be back within minutes, and she couldn't bear another of his scathing attacks. She walked around behind the breakfast bar, diluted the scalding coffee with cold water from the faucet, and downed a few bracing gulps.

She headed quietly down the hallway, toward the main entrance. She had almost reached it when a voice of authority stopped her.

"Jan!"

Reluctantly, feeling a small shiver of panic in reaction to the decisive voice, she glanced back over her shoulder. How could he have returned so quickly?

"Maria is taking care of Anton."

"Thank you for the coffee." Her voice was woodenly polite. "I'm fine now. Please let me know if there's anything I can do to help Anton."

Logan caught up with her and, before she could protest, he put himself as a formidable barrier between her and the door. "I tried to get hold of you at the station today. Everyone else was in a *Women's View* budget conference, but no one knew where you were."

Jan stated the obvious. "I was looking for Anton."

"I looked for him, too. I'm glad you succeeded where I failed." He paused, his eyes narrowed speculatively. "I suppose I'm surprised that you considered looking for Anton more important than the conference at the station. You left the field wide open for Stephanie. Or perhaps you forgot the conference?" he mocked lightly.

"No, I didn't forget it. It just didn't seem . . . essential."

"You don't consider your job at the station 'essential'?"

Jan considered the question slowly, turning and examining it as if it were a piece of the rainbow held within her hands. No, she didn't consider the job at the station, *Women's View*, or even a career in television *essential*. Important? Yes. She still wanted to put on the best show possible. She was willing to work hard for success. She still had ambitions toward moving upward to something bigger and better.

But she didn't want success at the price of sacrificing her personal integrity and standards, of becoming a female version of Paul Callison. She couldn't abandon her basic moral and ethical principles to get ahead. She didn't want success at the expense of damaging or cheating someone else. Not at Anton's expense. Not even at Stephanie's expense. Paul had said, "An idea belongs to the person who knows how to use it." He had made the statement sound righteous and necessary. But it wasn't. It was just another way of saying that the end justifies the means, that the goal of success justified any means of getting there. That wasn't a philosophy with which Jan could live. She could only work for success with honesty and fairness.

She swallowed convulsively. "I—I know you think I have no ethical or moral principles—"

He stepped forward and his hands shot out to lock her upper arms in a steel-trap grip. "I asked you a question about essentials."

Essentials? There was only one essential in her life. Logan. Since the door had closed on him last night, she felt as if she had been chopped in half. She was incomplete in a way less visible than the damage Anton and Mike had suffered, but no less devastating. She loved Logan. Even now as his hands bit ruthlessly into her arms and his blue eyes bored relentlessly into hers, she loved him.

And she had to escape before she humiliated herself by telling him so.

She wrenched one shoulder free, but he recaptured it immediately. "Please . . . please let me go." She knew she was begging but she no longer cared. She dropped her head wearily, then became aware it was resting on his shoulder, and jerked it up again.

"I told you I wanted to talk to you."

"And tell me again what you think of me?" Her defiance momentarily flared again. "Have you thought of a few more insulting words to throw at me? Wasn't the first list long enough?"

"Maybe it's your turn to throw a few." His left arm suddenly swept down to her waist and crushed her to him. "I might even help you think of a few appropriate terms if you'll stay with me."

Stay with me. The husky, softly spoken words were a sweet siren call of temptation. For a moment Jan allowed herself the luxury of drifting with them. To sleep in his arms with his body curved around hers . . . rouse drowsily in the night and feel the delicious warmth of his naked skin touching hers . . . wake at silvery dawn and see him as he still slept, his body lean and hard and tanned, uncompromisingly male, yet with a touch of boyish vulnerability too.

His lips touched her forehead, kisses as light as a caress of moonlight. "It's too late to drive back to Ventura tonight."

"It's only a short drive." Her words were aimed at herself more than at him as she tried to resist the languid feeling stealing over her. She mustn't stay . . . she really must not. This was just middle-of-the-night madness, and in the harsh light of morning they would both regret it. He was temporarily grateful to her, that was all. In the morning his fury and disgust would return.

His kisses moved down her temple to the sensitive angle just below her ear. She tilted her head back to give him access, telling herself *just a few moments more* before she pulled away. The kisses trailed across her throat and up to her other ear, seemingly without target until, with a fierce possessiveness, he suddenly claimed her mouth.

She resisted the demand of his tongue only momentarily before she bewitched herself with that same lulling *just a few moments more* thought. Just a few moments more of the taste and scent and male feel of him. This was all she would ever have, and she must hoard it up to last a lifetime.

His tongue explored her mouth like a conquerer returning to favorite haunts, and in spite of her weariness she felt whispery stirrings within her. His hand covered her breast, and it was she who moved restlessly, suddenly impatient with the barrier of clothing that separated her taut nipple from his caressing fingertips. If just for a moment she might feel the full warmth of his hand encompassing her breast without barrier between them . . .

As if in answer, his deft hand found a way beneath the barrier, answering one need, but waking another deeper and far more intimate one as some elemental core of her femininity responded.

And then it was too late. She had played with fire, postponed escape too long. He swept her up in his arms, his mouth still clamped to hers. To silence her protests? But there were no protests.

She was vaguely aware of lamp-lit room, a king-sized bed, rumpled, as if the former sole occupant had slept restlessly. She made some small gesture to aid in removal of her clothes, but his hands pushed hers away, and she was content to relax in the dreamy luxury of his attentions.

He kissed her again when they were naked in the bed, and she could feel the hard urgency of his male desire. But then, instead of sliding over her, he gently turned her on her side and snuggled her body into the protective arc of his. "Go to sleep, my sweet," he murmured softly.

She struggled to lift herself on one elbow, her head turned over her shoulder. "But I thought—I don't understand!" She could still feel the throb of his male need against her naked skin, yet he obviously intended to do nothing about it.

"Do you think I want you in my bed for only one reason? That's what you'll think if we make love now. Go to sleep. I want to hold you." He tucked his hand firmly around her breast.

Bewildered, Jan let herself slide back to the downy comfort of the pillow and into the secure curve of his body. She still felt a churning of fiery arousal deep within her body, still felt his need, yet she was too weary to try to figure it all out. Slowly the need in both of them subsided, replaced by a depth of intimate satisfaction that went beyond sex. How strange, Jan thought as she drifted into the final stages of sleep. How strange and bewildering . . .

Jan woke in near-darkness, thought she had slept only a few minutes, then realized that a beam of full sunlight was edging the heavy drapes. She sat up suddenly. The other half of the bed was empty, though from the looks of the covers they had both spent most of the night on the same side of the bed. She reached over and pulled a cord to open the drapes.

The bedside clock was the first thing she saw. Ten-thirty. *Ten-thirty!* She could have been at the station hours ago. She threw the covers back and just then the door opened. Logan walked in carrying a coffeepot and cups on a silver tray. He eyed her slim, naked body, poised as if for flight.

"Good morning."

"Good morning," Jan returned tentatively.

He set the tray on a bedside stand and opened another

set of drapes. Now Jan saw something else that surprised her. It was Anton's painting, *Legacy of Dawn*—the one with which she had come precariously close to collision at the art exhibit.

"You bought it?"

Logan glanced at the impressive painting and nodded. "It was our introduction, remember? Maybe I'm sentimental."

He glanced back at her, and she felt suddenly shy at being naked while he was fully clothed. She retreated to the bed and pulled a corner of the sheet over her. He followed and gently but decisively removed the sheet. Then, as if he were greeting them good-morning, just as he had greeted her, he leaned over and kissed the rosy tip of first one breast and then the other. Jan felt the same bewildered confusion she had felt last night.

"About last night," she began tentatively. "When you asked me to stay—"

"My tactics were a bit unethical, weren't they?" he reflected. "But you wouldn't have stayed unless I used a physical persuasion." He smiled, a familiar, slightly wicked gleam in his eyes that made Jan's heart lurch.

"But—"

"Do you know why I bought that particular painting of Anton's? I wanted it to be a small wedding present for you."

Jan felt faint. "You don't need to be cruel."

He eyed the painting again. "I still do," he added matter-of-factly. When she made no response, he gave her an oblique look. "That's a backhanded sort of proposal, if you're interested."

Interested? Jan's heart felt as if it had sprouted wings. But just as quickly she thudded back to earth. "I—I love you, Logan. I guess I always will. But there would always be this thing with Anton between us. I made a mistake. Several mistakes. You'll never know how sorry I am, but it's done, and there's no changing the damage it did Anton." The broken words trailed off. She felt a chasm widen slowly between them.

"I don't think the damage is irreparable. He's much better

this morning," Logan said slowly. "But there's always the unpleasant possibility that his recovery will take much longer than it would have if the show hadn't set him back."

Jan sat there, very still and quiet. Is this how you feel, she wondered, when heaven comes within your grasp . . . and then slips away?

"But even if that happens, I'll still love you," Logan said with no trace of doubt. "You made a mistake. We all do. I made one yesterday when in anger I called you things I had no right to. But it's what a person does *after* a mistake is made that really counts, what you do to try to correct it. I called you hard all the way through. But now I'm beginning to realize that what you have is a steel core of courage and determination to correct a mistake. That's part of the reason I love you." He paused and smiled lightly. "But I'm rather fond of some of the exterior trimmings around that steel core, too." He ran his hand lightly across the smooth plane of her abdomen.

"I love you," Jan said helplessly.

He pushed her back against the bed. "Prove it," he whispered huskily.

She twined her fingers in his hair and kissed him, exploring the warm interior of his mouth with her tongue and arching her body to meet his, trying in every way she knew to show him how much she loved him.

"Pretty good," he admitted. "But not good enough."

She felt the sinking pangs of failure.

"I'm the old-fashioned type. Nothing less than marriage will be proof enough for me."

"If you insist," Jan agreed, laughter and relief bubbling in her voice.

"But in the meantime," he said obligingly as he fit his body more intimately against hers, "you're welcome to offer such other actions of evidence as you might care to—"

Jan cut him off with a kiss.

Second Chance at Love

_____ 05703-7 **FLAMENCO NIGHTS #1** Susanna Collins

_____ 05637-5 **WINTER LOVE SONG #2** Meredith Kingston

_____ 05624-3 **THE CHADBOURNE LUCK #3** Lucia Curzon

_____ 05777-0 **OUT OF A DREAM #4** Jennifer Rose

_____ 05878-5 **GLITTER GIRL #5** Jocelyn Day

_____ 05863-7 **AN ARTFUL LADY #6** Sabina Clark

_____ 05694-4 **EMERALD BAY #7** Winter Ames

_____ 05776-2 **RAPTURE REGAINED #8** Serena Alexander

_____ 05801-7 **THE CAUTIOUS HEART #9** Philippa Heywood

_____ 05907-2 **ALOHA YESTERDAY #10** Meredith Kingston

_____ 05638-3 **MOONFIRE MELODY #11** Lily Bradford

_____ 06132-8 **MEETING WITH THE PAST #12** Caroline Halter

_____ 05623-5 **WINDS OF MORNING #13** Laurie Marath

_____ 05704-5 **HARD TO HANDLE #14** Susanna Collins

_____ 06067-4 **BELOVED PIRATE #15** Margie Michaels

_____ 05978-1 **PASSION'S FLIGHT #16** Marilyn Mathieu

_____ 05847-5 **HEART OF THE GLEN #17** Lily Bradford

_____ 05977-3 **BIRD OF PARADISE #18** Winter Ames

_____ 05705-3 **DESTINY'S SPELL #19** Susanna Collins

_____ 06106-9 **GENTLE TORMENT #20** Johanna Phillips

_____ 06059-3 **MAYAN ENCHANTMENT #21** Lila Ford

_____ 06301-0 **LED INTO SUNLIGHT #22** Claire Evans

_____ 06131-X **CRYSTAL FIRE #23** Valerie Nye

_____ 06150-6 **PASSION'S GAMES #24** Meredith Kingston

_____ 06160-3 **GIFT OF ORCHIDS #25** Patti Moore

_____ 06108-5 **SILKEN CARESSES #26** Samantha Carroll

_____ 06318-5 **SAPPHIRE ISLAND #27** Diane Crawford

_____ 06335-5 **APHRODITE'S LEGEND #28** Lynn Fairfax

_____ 06336-3 **TENDER TRIUMPH #29** Jasmine Craig

_____ 06280-4 **AMBER-EYED MAN #30** Johanna Phillips

_____ 06249-9 **SUMMER LACE #31** Jenny Nolan

_____ 06305-3 **HEARTTHROB #32** Margarett McKean

_____ 05626-X **AN ADVERSE ALLIANCE #33** Lucia Curzon

_____ 06162-X **LURED INTO DAWN #34** Catherine Mills

Second Chance at Love

_____ 06195-6 SHAMROCK SEASON #35 Jennifer Rose

_____ 06304-5 HOLD FAST TIL MORNING #36 Beth Brookes

_____ 06282-0 HEARTLAND #37 Lynn Fairfax

_____ 06408-4 FROM THIS DAY FORWARD #38 Jolene Adams

_____ 05968-4 THE WIDOW OF BATH #39 Anne Devon

_____ 06400-9 CACTUS ROSE #40 Zandra Colt

_____ 06401-7 PRIMITIVE SPLENDOR #41 Katherine Swinford

_____ 06424-6 GARDEN OF SILVERY DELIGHTS #42 Sharon Francis

_____ 06521-8 STRANGE POSSESSION #43 Johanna Phillips

_____ 06326-6 CRESCENDO #44 Melinda Harris

_____ 05818-1 INTRIGUING LADY #45 Daphne Woodward

_____ 06547-1 RUNAWAY LOVE #46 Jasmine Craig

_____ 06423-8 BITTERSWEET REVENGE #47 Kelly Adams

_____ 06541-2 STARBURST #48 Tess Ewing

_____ 06540-4 FROM THE TORRID PAST #49 Ann Cristy

_____ 06544-7 RECKLESS LONGING #50 Daisy Logan

_____ 05851-3 LOVE'S MASQUERADE #51 Lillian Marsh

_____ 06148-4 THE STEELE HEART #52 Jocelyn Day

_____ 06422-X UNTAMED DESIRE #53 Beth Brookes

_____ 06651-6 VENUS RISING #54 Michelle Roland

_____ 06595-1 SWEET VICTORY #55 Jena Hunt

_____ 06575-7 TOO NEAR THE SUN #56 Aimée Duvall

All of the above titles are $1.75 per copy

_____ 05625-1 **MOURNING BRIDE #57** Lucia Curzon

_____ 06411-4 **THE GOLDEN TOUCH #58** Robin James

_____ 06596-X **EMBRACED BY DESTINY #59** Simone Hadary

_____ 06660-5 **TORN ASUNDER #60** Ann Cristy

_____ 06573-0 **MIRAGE #61** Margie Michaels

_____ 06650-8 **ON WINGS OF MAGIC #62** Susanna Collins

_____ 05816-5 **DOUBLE DECEPTION #63** Amanda Troy

_____ 06675-3 **APOLLO'S DREAM #64** Claire Evans

_____ 06676-1 **SMOLDERING EMBERS #65** Marie Charles

_____ 06677-X **STORMY PASSAGE #66** Laurel Blake

_____ 06678-8 **HALFWAY THERE #67** Aimée Duvall

_____ 06679-6 **SURPRISE ENDING #68** Elinor Stanton

_____ 06680-X **THE ROGUE'S LADY #69** Anne Devon

_____ 06681-8 **A FLAME TOO FIERCE #70** Jan Mathews

_____ 06682-6 **SATIN AND STEELE #71** Jaelyn Conlee

_____ 06683-4 **MIXED DOUBLES #72** Meredith Kingston

_____ 06684-2 **RETURN ENGAGEMENT #73** Kay Robbins

_____ 06685-0 **SULTRY NIGHTS #74** Ariel Tierney

_____ 06686-9 **AN IMPROPER BETROTHMENT #75** Henrietta Houston

_____ 06687-7 **FORSAKING ALL OTHERS #76** LaVyrle Spencer

_____ 06688-5 **BEYOND PRIDE #77** Kathleen Ash

_____ 06689-3 **SWEETER THAN WINE #78** Jena Hunt

_____ 06690-7 **SAVAGE EDEN #79** Diane Crawford

_____ 06691-5 **STORMY REUNION #80** Jasmine Craig

_____ 06692-3 **THE WAYWARD WIDOW #81** Anne Mayfield

_____ 06693-1 **TARNISHED RAINBOW #82** Jocelyn Day

_____ 06694-X **STARLIT SEDUCTION #83** Anne Reed

_____ 06695-8 **LOVER IN BLUE #84** Aimée Duvall

_____ 06696-6 **THE FAMILIAR TOUCH #85** Lynn Lawrence

_____ 06697-4 **TWILIGHT EMBRACE #86** Jennifer Rose

_____ 06698-2 **QUEEN OF HEARTS #87** Lucia Curzon

All of the above titles are $1.75 per copy

WHAT READERS SAY ABOUT
SECOND CHANCE AT LOVE BOOKS

"Your books are the greatest!"
 —*M. N., Carteret, New Jersey**

"I have been reading romance novels for quite some time, but the SECOND CHANCE AT LOVE books are the most enjoyable."
 —*P. R., Vicksburg, Mississippi**

"I enjoy SECOND CHANCE [AT LOVE] more than any books that I have read and I do read a lot."
 —*J. R., Gretna, Louisiana**

"For years I've had my subscription in to Harlequin. Currently there is a series called Circle of Love, but you have them all beat."
 —*C. B., Chicago, Illinois**

"I really think your books are exceptional... I read Harlequin and Silhouette and although I still like them, I'll buy your books over theirs. SECOND CHANCE [AT LOVE] is more interesting and holds your attention and imagination with a better story line..."
 —*J. W., Flagstaff, Arizona**

"I've read many romances, but yours take the 'cake'!"
 —*D. H., Bloomsburg, Pennsylvania**

"Have waited ten years for *good* romance books. Now I have them."
 —*M. P., Jacksonville, Florida**

*Names and addresses available upon request